Decomposition
by J Eric Miller

Decomposition
Decomposition
Decomposition
Decomposition
Decomposition
Decomposition
Dec mposition
Decompesition
Deco   position
Decomposition
Decomposition

ecompositlonDecompositionn

Decomposition
Decomposition
Decomqosition
D com,,,position

Decomposition

Becomposition
Decomposi.tion
Decomposition
Deco**mpo**sition
Decomposition
Decomposition
Deco..sitidfdon
Decomooisition
Decomposition
Decosfsscvition
Decomposi tion
Devcoinsdfffon
De**po**mgggbn
Dec.d fdfffn
De   sition
Decof..,,n

By J E nm
y J% Mieler
By) Er..gjille
By Jll Eric r
By J Er--=-*M*iller
By JJ Er tgMiller
By rixc Md ller
By J *Ersdic* Miller
By I Effffnbric Mooer

By J Eric Miller

By J EddfdfMill ller
De gc J Eric Miller
By J EddddMiller
By J Eric Miller
By JJJric Miller
Be J Erie Miller
By J Eric Miller
By J Eric .jh,6iller
By Jeric Mller
By T Eric Miller
By Eric Miller
By J Eric Miller
By J Eric Miller
By J Er ic Miller
By J Eric Miller
By J Eric Miller
By J Eric Miller
By J Eric Miller

EPHEMERA BOUND PUBLISHING, FARGO ND

Decomposition ©2005 J Eric Miller

All characters and events in this book are completely fictional. Any resemblance to real people, living or dead, is purely coincidental.

"Mustang" is a trademark of Ford Motor Co., which does not endorse, nor is affiliated with this book.

Special thanks to Craig Johnson and Tim Dahlsad for access to the beautiful Ford Mustang featured on the cover.

Book design, cover photomosaic by Derek Dahlsad
This edition ©2006 Equilibri-Yum Inc

Ephemera Bound Publishing
A Divison of Equilibri-Yum Incorporated
719 9th St N
Fargo ND 58102
http://www.ephemera-bound.com

Library of Congress Cataloging-in-Publication Data

Miller, J. Eric.
    Decomposition / by J. Eric Miller.
        p. cm.
    ISBN-13: 978-0-9771003-8-5 (pbk. : alk. paper)
    1. Women murderers--Fiction. 2. Man-woman relationships--Fiction.
3. Psychological fiction. I. Title.
    PS3613.I537D43 2006
    813'.6--dc22

                                                    2006006893

0 9 8 7 6 5 4 3 2 1

For Jodi Hass, as always.

With special thanks to Barb Gerhardt
for a final and good pair of eyes.

Decomposition

George was a good boyfriend and I didn't kill him; but I broke his heart. He bought me this Mustang and when I finally get to Seattle, I'll pull up in it and he'll come running down his front porch steps and lean through the window and kiss me. Then everything will be fine.

Before I get there, I have to figure out what to do with Jack. He's the bad boyfriend, the one I did kill.

This is the first road trip of my life, and I've got to get him out of the trunk sometime before it's over.

Here are the things to hate about New Orleans: wet heat; insects; decay.

Why I thought I could make a home in a place that stinks of sweat and mold and death, I don't know.

Why I left George in Atlanta to be with Jack in a place like this, I can't explain. Anyway, I don't need to explain, or even really know.

They tell you to think about what is in front of you, not what is behind.

I've never been to Seattle, but I know it will be the kind of place I can stay.

From here I just go north and west. Really, it can't be simpler.

They say the hurricane is going to raise the sea to bury this city. So it should. I'll be long gone.

I don't want a map of this journey. I've had enough of structure. Jack was a writer and a professor, and he had little maps for everything: how a day should go; how his classes should go; how the stories he was writing should go.

When things didn't work out as he'd planned them, Jack could be a real asshole.

Shame on you, Jack.

I know that after dawn, these empty roads are going to fill up with all the people who will flee the hurricane. Where they'll go, I don't know, but I'm sure none of them will make it as far away as I will.

I suppose they have most of their lives to pack up. I've brought very little: toothpaste and a brush, two changes of clothes, a makeup case.

And Jack.

Maybe I should have left him.

George is soft, is nothing like Jack. He might not be the most handsome man in the world, he might not have any of the edges that a guy like Jack has, but George is good in the simple way people mean the word. I should have known the first time that he was right for me, but I was too young to know much of anything then.

Anyway, because of what happened to Danny Boy, I wasn't ready for what George had to offer. Now I am.

Jack was strong and vital and handsome. These are just secret poisons. They make a man attractive, but they also make him incapable of really loving. Jack wanted to possess me, but he never tried to really know me. He wanted me to be his private audience and admire him.

What do you think of your fan club now, Jack?

Five hours ago, he was still alive.

I was still his prisoner.

I was still addicted to the idea of his affection and the feel of his cock.

Jack was just a habit.

And breaking it like this is exciting.

What's going on now, it's a love story, kind of. And in it, I'm my own hero. If there was a dragon, it was Jack, and I had to slay him myself and escape the cave in which he kept me. In this fairy tale, George is kind of like the sleeping beauty.

And the sun comes up and I'm racing along like this, wondering if I'll make it.

North and west.

I've just got to get really rid of Jack.

Decomposition

The interstate is busy. A car comes flashing past and zips in front of me. When I brake, I hear the weight of Jack shifting in the trunk. He's got on a bathrobe and pajama bottoms and no shirt. His eyes, the last time I saw them, were open, but you could see in them that he was dead.

Jack's the first person I killed, but he's not the first dead person I've seen. I saw my own son dead. I saw other people, too, including my mother's parents, who died in a car accident and had their bodies displayed one beside the other at the funeral home.

They say that when people die you learn something, and maybe that is true.

One morning at a café where Jack was reading his newspaper, two men on the sidewalk came past us. One of the men had a bow pulled taut and the arrow tip against the back of the other man's skull. The guy with the bow kept muttering, "Get on now, get on..." The other guy was little Black man in a seersucker suit and he never looked side-to-side but just straight down in front of him as if he were worried about tripping. Jack was annoyed that I'd followed him down to the café; he'd looked over the top of his newspaper and told me I'd broken the ritual of his Sunday morning coffee and read and now something bad was going to happen. Then he disappeared into the newspaper and it wasn't long after that the two men appeared on the sidewalk. A man next to Jack and me had gotten up when he saw the situation. At what seemed like the right time, he leapt over the little café fence and knocked the bow and arrow guy down. For a moment, I thought everything was going to be fine. Then I saw the Black man was swaying back and forth and that the feathered part of the arrow was standing out from the back of his head and that the point was somewhere inside of it. He still didn't look at anything but the sidewalk. He fell forward. A wrinkly woman in a flower print dress came running up to the shot man and dipped a white handkerchief in the blood that ran out around the arrow.

Jack threw up.

I took his hand and helped him to his feet as he dabbed at his face with a napkin. After a moment, he started to lead me away. I wanted to ask him what the woman wanted with the blood, but I could smell his vomit and I realized there was no real way he'd know the answer to that question.

In fact, I realized right then that he didn't know as much about anything as he wanted me to think he did.

I can't seem to keep my foot heavy on the pedal. I tell it to push and for a moment it goes down and then it just seems to forget.

I want to look at him.

I can feel a pressure building in my stomach and chest, and I know the only way to release it is to pull over. Open the trunk. Make sure he's dead.

Of course, there is more to this need than that.

Who knows what it really is that makes me want to look at him? And anyway, who wants to know everything?

It's a stupid move on a busy interstate, but you can't do the smart thing all the time. Sometimes, you take chances. Like killing Jack. Like the cavemen, playing with fire for the good it would bring them. Like the Americans, crossing the country against all those bears and Indians and loneliness.

Cars and trucks and SUVs whizzing by on both sides. I try to get over, but somebody honks and I have to jerk back into my own lane.

Keep your head, I tell myself.

Don't shut down, I tell myself.

Just put on your blinker and sooner or later somebody will let you over.

Horns and people pumping up their fingers and some fat blond woman screaming at me through the passenger side glass.

I see and hear all this the way you see and hear things on a television screen.

Then I've made it, by accident and luck, and I'm pulling off alongside the road, braking to a slow stop. I'm sort of shaky and I go around the front of the Mustang and down the passenger side and then try to position my body between what will be the open trunk and the viewpoint of the passing cars.

I take a deep breath, and, in releasing it, I realize how tired I am.

Decomposition

Then I open the lid.

Jack's knees are tucked up and over, and his back is flat on the trunk floor. His face has come out of the sheet I wrapped him in. Bloody goop is oozing out of one of his nostrils and there is blood on his teeth. I use the sheet to dab it away and that makes him look better. He has a perplexed expression on his face, as if he is thinking about something that bothers him.

Beyond that, perhaps he is more pale than normal. Perhaps the color is faded in his lips a bit. Basically, you can tell he's dead, even though you can't tell anything that has happened to him. There is an overall appearance of stiffness to him. I know this is *rigor mortis*. I took two biology courses and learned about the stage of decomposition. I know that already the bacteria that used to feed on the contents of Jack's intestines are now feeding on the large intestine itself. I know that soon they will have eaten their way through it and will start eating the organs that surround it.

They've been saving up all their gluttony for this exact time. The feast of Jack.

It won't last long before they'll eat everything there is to eat. Then Jack will really be gone.

In the class we watched sped up videos of a baby pig de-composing. I don't know how it died, but after I'd watched it puff up with gasses and pulse with insects as if it was trying to come back to life, I felt close to it, like it had been my own little pet and was tied to me in a special way. Then we watched it start to rot away.

It made me think of Danny Boy.

That was when I stopped eating bacon and pork chops and anything else that came from a pig.

I'm standing still too long. There is just the sound of the traffic on the interstate, and the insects in the tall grass alongside of it.

I don't want flies and their eggs and the maggots from those eggs to infest the trunk of my car.

Jack deserved his death, but I don't even want them to infest him.

There's insect repellent in the glove compartment. I close the trunk and look up and down the road at the passing cars and I see no sign of anybody having noticed anything, all these people who probably can't even imagine finding their ways into a fairy tale.

I used to be one of them. Or maybe not. Maybe I was never like everybody else.

I get out the bottle of repellent and shake it as I walk back down the car. Then I open the trunk again and spray all over the sheet that covers Jack and finally work my nerve up to squirt his face. The sheen on his cheeks and forehead and the tip of his nose shimmers for a moment and then seems to sink in.

The bottle is almost empty, and I use what is left to spray the inside of the trunk and then the lid after I close it.

This hassle with Jack, it was avoidable.

I know I could have left him in the apartment, and then the water they say is coming could have swept him away.

Then it would have been just me and my Mustang on the road to George.

I suppose I wasn't ready for that.

But I will leave you, Jack.

And I think of the girl, Kimberly, that student of his who made him laugh at her when she moved into a house across the way. Or maybe it was that he was laughing at me because I said she was trying to be close to him. She moved in and I said to Jack that he ought to be careful, and he looked out the window at her unloading boxes and he laughed. Kimberly, her light, it came on late last night, just as I was backing out of the garage with Jack in the trunk of the car.

As I drive, I can't help wondering what kind of coincidence, or lack of coincidence, that was.

This pretty country road.

If nothing changes inside of me or outside of me between now and Seattle, I'll make it.

The wheel is steady in my hands and the pedal is fine under my foot and all of this is good. I've turned north on a highway,

Decomposition

where only a little traffic has trickled off the main flow. Trees are hanging over the road, and half the sky is light blue. I feel like I could drive for nearly ever.

So Seattle should be a breeze.

Of course, I know it won't go like that.

Every yellow brick road passes through a few dark forests.

To get to the happy end of this fairy tale, I've got to make my way past a few obstacles. What you lose on them is what you trade for what you get.

Jack taught students how to write stories. I know all about protagonists. I know all about proving journeys.

I'll make it. I can. I will.

If I didn't need gas, I'd not stop driving until I reached Seattle.

But this isn't one of those magic stories where you get to break the laws of nature.

I pull off at a cluster of buildings. Amongst them is a gas station with those old fashioned pumps, and across the road from it is a diner. In the parking lot of the gas station is a truck with metal sides and hand-sized holes cut into them. I think it is the kind that they usually use to haul pigs, but this one is full of chickens. There must be more than three hundred of them jammed in there, dirty and sick looking.

At first I just want to ignore it, but I can't.

They must be going from one dark shed to another, cramped and miserable and waiting to die. I think it would be better if the truck just blew up and the chickens just went into blackness.

I can't make the truck blow up.

I can't make anything good happen for them.

There is nothing to do but go and pump my gas. It has a clean smell I've always liked. Inside, there is only a woman behind the counter. She's old and fat and has curly gray hair.

"You see that truck out there?" I ask her.

"Yep."

"It's kind of a shame."

She doesn't say anything, but I can tell she doesn't think it's a shame. I can tell she doesn't think about anything. She's probably worked here all her life—she might even own the place—but she doesn't like it. Maybe once she thought somebody would save her, or maybe she always knew she'd have to save herself if she were to be saved at all.

I pay for my gas and leave.

Before I get into my car, I have an idea. It is that even though I can't blow up the truck, and even though I can't rescue all the chickens, I can save one from all that misery.

In this story, not only am I my own heroine, but I rescue others as well.

I go to the back of the truck and some of the chickens look up at me. They're all pretty much alike and I don't want to try to make a choice, so I plan to just reach in and grab randomly. Then we'll run.

When George comes down the steps of his house and leans in my car window and kisses me, I'll say, "Look who I brought."

He'll smile.

There is no lock, just an old bolt jammed down into the latch. I have to hit it with the palm of my hand several times before it loosens and comes up. When I see that my palm has been torn bloody, I feel calmer, as if I've paid my price and it's not that awful.

The door opens with a creak, and it opens wider than I mean it to. About half the chickens come to life. Several of them stand up and start clucking and beating their wings. Before I can think to do anything, two chickens leap through the open doorway. Now about half the chickens are pushing against each other and clucking.

"Shhhhh," I say, even though I know it won't do any good.

The two that have jumped out are walking around. I'll put the first one I catch back and keep the second one, but before I can do anything else, there is a bigger commotion inside the trailer. A chicken leaps from right in the middle of the mess of them and slaps into the steel siding and falls back amongst the others. Several more jump and a couple of these make it out of the truck. Now those that are out are running all over the place. One chicken has perched in the doorway and I get my hands around the outside of her wings and hold them against her body so that she can't hit me with them. Then I stand there for a second feeling her heart beat. Three or four more chickens jump out. I see that several are moving toward the road.

"No!" I scream. This causes more of a flurry inside the truck, and from this flurry comes a fresh burst of chickens so that I have to duck out of their way. The foremost chicken dashes into the road. A car hits her and she flies a ways and lands right on the yellow line and the same car that hit her now runs over her. There's another car behind it, and a truck coming from the opposite direction. I close my eyes and hear the thunks. Chickens dash around squawking and the chickens still in the truck are squawking and the chicken I'm holding squawks.

For a moment, I try to make it all a dream.

More chickens run into the road. Horns blare. The squawking gets louder. Most drivers don't even slow and none of them stops after hitting chickens. There are dead chickens everywhere and live chickens running around and there are some chickens that have been hit but are not dead.

A bright blue car comes skidding through the mess of blood and feathers. The car brakes and slides off the road and runs into a telephone pole at the far end of the parking lot of the diner. A middle-aged man in a Hawaiian shirt gets out.

"What the hell?" It's as if he asking the chickens. Some of them have made it across the road without being hit and are clucking around the bodies of chickens that have.

Out of the diner comes the man who must be the driver of the chicken truck. He's got a napkin in his shirt and a drumstick in his hand. The chickens that made it to that side run from him back into the road. Another car speeds through, sending two or three chickens into the air. The truck driver begins to swing his drumstick around, trying to herd chickens off the road. They go this way and that way, but none of the ways he seems to want them to. He kicks one and she flies straight up in the air and then lands on the asphalt. After a moment, she tries to get up but can't.

The guy in the Hawaiian shirt is yelling at the driver of the truck.

A bus is coming. I run with the chicken I'm holding to my car and put her in the passenger seat, and then I get in the other side. The driver waves his arms as the bus arrives, and the bus driver honks and brakes. The tires burst dead and half dead chickens. A car behind the bus rams into it. The man in the Hawaiian shirt runs toward the driver of the chicken truck and swings at him. The driver ducks away and then drops his drumstick and punches the man. Blood shoots from the man's nose, and the man wobbles a few steps and then falls backward into the dirt parking lot. I hear more glass breaking and more metal crumpling, but I don't look to see who has hit what. I pull backwards fast. The wheels squeal and then I start forward, keeping my eyes wide so as not to run over any chickens.

Then I'm on the road, going north again.

If I were a weaker person I'd tell myself that this was all fated and that it was supposed to be just this one chicken to escape that hell on the road, or that hell in which they had been living and were going to die.

But I don't believe that this is anybody's plan.

I know that in trying to do something good I made a mistake and might have made things worse.

Maybe a weaker person would throw out this one chicken because she'd see it as a memento to failure.

But I'm not a weaker person. I make this journey in strength.

I'll keep what I should and let go of what I ought to, and I'll be just fine.

The chicken stands on the seat and sort of wobbles. Her head cocks and I see that she is looking at me with an orange eye. I didn't know chickens have orange eyes. Maybe they don't. Maybe it's just her. She blinks. I blink back at her. I try cocking my head so that she thinks she is in the company of somebody who is like her.

"What shall we call you?"

She clucks, as if she has understood the question and thinks it an appropriate one.

"I'll call you Little Dear," I say. That was the name of a chicken in a book my father read me when I was little.

I tell this one, the real Little Dear, about the story we're in and the parts we'll play; I tell her about the journey we're on and that it will end in Seattle.

She cranes her head and blinks. I know that really she can't understand me, but I feel understood just the same.

When Danny Boy first began to speak, it was like magic to me.

She doesn't try to move her head away when I reach to touch it. Even though it's all feathers, it feels dry.

"Jack was like a lot of men," I tell Little Dear. "First he wanted to fuck and fuck and fuck me. Then he wanted to fuck me in all these strange ways. And then he stopped wanting to fuck me altogether."

I know she's not really nodding, but her head bobs up and down as if she is.

I put my hand on her back, where the feathers are softer, and I tell her we are driving towards George. I tell her that what we've done back at the gas station and the diner might make people come after us.

"We're going north," I tell her, "But I'll take another road when we can. We'll go west for a while. You'll see that everything can be just fine."

We drive.

It's hot in the car and Little Dear has her beak open. Her lid is halfway down her eye. I turn on the air conditioning.

My father used to get drunk two or three times a year, and then he'd seek me out and talk quietly and slowly with me until my mother caught him. Sometimes even after I left, he'd do the same. He called me half a year ago in New Orleans and I could hear he had been drinking. He told me that sex is like food and less essential than love, which he said is like water, without which one will quickly die. "Even Gandhi," he said, "drank water while he fasted."

Maybe he was telling me about himself and my mother, or maybe he was trying to tell me something about me and Jack, or me and George. Maybe he wasn't trying to tell me anything. Maybe he was just talking to talk.

That was the last time I spoke with my father.

That was before they cut off his foot.

I'm thirsty. Little Dear too, I imagine.

A gas station always appears just when you need one to.

This one has large windows that reflect, and everything is white or blue. A man who looks like Mr. Rogers is sweeping outside, smiling as if he enjoys his work. There is a sense of freshness to the place, like it could never be old and never be dirty. It looks like a gas station on the moon, or in a book for children. Just past it, the road passes over an interstate that runs east and west.

"Exactly what we needed," I tell Little Dear.

I go inside and first find a diet soda. My figure is important to me. Jack was as caught up in his body as I am in mine. He'd go to the gym for an hour five days a week, and every night he'd do a thousand sit-ups. He'd ask me to trace the lines in between his stomach muscles. He'd ask me to grip his arms. At first I wanted to feed his vanity, but then I begin to notice that he never fed mine, so I tried to admire him only in secret.

"You're in great shape for a thirty-five-year-old man," I told him once.

He said, "One doesn't go into the world and compete with other thirty-five- old men. One just competes with men."

I asked him what he was competing for.

There was a right answer. It was me.

What he said was: "For everything."

I know how men think. They think the woman with them is one they've only had to win once.

Sunflower seeds, a bottle of water, a soda: four dollars and seventy nine cents.

Credit card, my name, but Jack's account.

Outside of the gas station is an empty police car. I flash an image of a cop standing beside the Mustang with his gun raised and pointed at Little Dear's head.

This is just guilt-induced paranoia. This is just me caving a little against the pressure.

Decomposition

The cop is not beside my car. He must be somewhere inside, perhaps watching me through the glass.

I'm telling myself to play it cool, but I can't stop myself from running. Just as I reach the Mustang, the police officer comes out of the gas station. A blond man with a young face, he turns directly to me. I look away. When I look back, he snaps his fingers and turns and goes back into the gas station.

I open the passenger door quickly.

"It's ok."

Little Dear clucks.

I pick her up. One of her wings gets out from under my fingers and I feel tendons and muscles' jerking before the wing comes down hard against my cheek. I understand that she doesn't know what is happening. Her trust level is low; it should be. It will take a while before she knows that all I want to do is help her.

"It's okay," I say again. I re-grip the wing. I have to hold her harder than I'd like and can feel her bones bend a little under my fingers. She turns her head to the side and looks up at me with that orange eye. I walk quickly to the back of the car and open the trunk. Jack looks much the same as before, perhaps stiffer—but maybe I'm just imaging that because I know he ought to have hardened more by now. In any case, I have the urge to touch his face and make sure that it feels like flesh.

There is no time for that.

The officer is coming back out of the gas station.

I put Little Dear down beside Jack.

The officer is holding a soda he didn't have the first time he came out, and he doesn't look at me as he twists the top of it off. There are other people in the lot and I glance at them to see if anybody has noticed that I put a chicken in my trunk or that there is a body in it with her. Little Dear and Jack, my secrets. As far as I can tell, everybody is going about their lives as if everything is normal.

For now, I envy them.

I close the lid and the officer looks at me. He smiles as I move down the car and open the driver side door and get in.

I start the car and he's still looking at me.

He must see that I'm pretty. I imagine he thinks about fucking me. I'm not one of those girls that is bothered by men wanting them. I've known plenty of girls that men didn't want to fuck, and that's worth getting upset about.

I smile back. He's twirling his keys around his finger. He keeps walking and then stops to take a drink of his soda, and after he swallows, he looks at me again. Then he gets in his car.

He seems to be watching me as I drive, and he pulls out behind me.

As I drive, I tell myself to calm. I am approaching the intersection that would put me on the westbound interstate. I jerk the wheel and hit the turn signal and veer to the right and onto the ramp. The officer turns, just at the last moment, the way I did.

He's following me.

Or maybe he's just going the same direction I am.

My face is sweaty in the rear view mirror and I see a little swollen purple mark where Little Dear hit me. I could use a handkerchief and a few seconds with my compact. I could use a long shower. A blow dryer and a hair curler.

I could use a lot of things.

I try not to look at the police car behind me or the officer in it.

He follows me for two or three miles. Then he speeds up a little and pulls into the left lane. Alongside of me, he slows and looks over. I smile at him. Smiling at people is what I've done all my life.

"Prettiness is a poison," my mother used to tell me. "People think that pretty people owe them things." It's the kind of thing unattractive people tell themselves, but my mother was not one of those; she was pretty and still is, sort of.

I think the reason she said things like that is because she never wanted me to be pretty.

The officer is still alongside of me. I tell myself that if he pulls me over it will be because of my smile. If he pulls me over, I'll do anything to keep him from looking in the trunk. I'll fuck him, even, if it will keep my journey from ending. We could fuck in the back seat of one of our cars. He would be the last lover I have before returning to George. His cock could be something to clear away the soil of Jack in me.

I glance over at the officer. He is staring straight ahead, his jaw line sharp. Then he turns and looks at me. His eyes appear very blue.

He could keep his badge on. He could keep his hat on, too. I smile in a way I imagine will say all of this to him. A look I can't read crosses his face. Then he nods his head and speeds up, passing me.

The interstate is posted 65, but he's going faster. I wonder about the strange look he gave me. Perhaps he didn't see my smile, or maybe he misunderstood it. I have the urge to check my face again, to make sure everything is all right. I speed up to 70 to come up behind his car. It's impossible to tell if he looks at me or not in his rear view mirror. We drive like this for a mile or two. His car slowly pulls away from mine. Soon, he is well ahead of me. I speed up to 75 and then 80. When I get close again, I can see that he has put on dark sunglasses.

He could keep those on, too. I think I'd come in just a few minutes. He could come as well and that would be that.

We're going 85 now. His brake lights redden. I swerve around him. Now he's following me. I speed up even more. His car gets small behind me and I feel a pang of disappointment that he's let me leave him behind.

Then I see he is gaining on me. When he is close, his siren lets out a short burst and the lights come on. He won't have to say anything. Maybe he can fuck me on the trunk of my car.

What would you think of that, Jack?

I pull over. The officer pulls over behind me. I smooth my hair and use the hem of my sundress to wipe my face. Though the officer is not out of his car, I roll down my window. I see him talking into his radio. This makes me wonder if it is possible that somebody knows about Jack and that the officer is now finding out about what I've done.

Kimberly, that student, with her lights coming on just as I was leaving, maybe she saw something. Maybe she found the blood inside the house or some other evidence and called the police with a description of my car.

Or perhaps the cop is finding out about what I did with the chicken truck, and this will lead him to search my trunk.

There are any number of reasons he might want to open it.

Even if he does, when I tell him the story of why I killed Jack, he'll understand. He'll still want to fuck me. We will fuck in a way which clears both of us of our pasts. Then he will drive one way and I will drive another.

He gets out and comes toward me. When he reaches the window, I wait for him to lean down, but he doesn't.

"Ma'am, did you not notice the speed limit signs?"

"Was I speeding?"

"You were up to 91 in 65. It's posted. I thought maybe you might not know because you saw I was right there." His voice is pleasant, but distant, like he's reading a letter for a blind person.

"I didn't realize I was speeding."

"Are you all right, ma'am?"

"Of course I am." I give a little laugh. I want to call him "silly" or something like that, but I don't. I just smile up at him. He is studying me in the wrong way, squinting his eyes and frowning.

I wonder what it is that is the matter with him.

"May I see your license and registration and insurance?"

"Of course."

My hands are shaky as I hand over the things he's asked for.

"Thank you," he says. Then he walks back to his car.

For a little while, I don't know what to make of any of this. Then it comes to me that he must be homosexual. I feel like calling him "faggot" in my mind, but that is just an angry impulse, and I can be bigger than it.

When he comes back, it is with a ticket on a clipboard.

"Please sign this."

"Ok."

"I'm sorry to do this," he says. "I tried to give you warning and an opportunity to slow down. I wrote it at 79. It won't be so bad."

"Thank you," I say. I think it must be hard to be a homosexual police officer. He must have to hide it from the other cops. His secret life is probably eating away at him all the time. After he gives me a copy of my ticket and my license and registration and insurance back, I wait for him to pull back onto the highway, but he does not. I realize that I am supposed to go first, and so I do. Then I watch as he crosses the meridian and goes back in the direction from which he came.

Poor man. There is nobody to save him.

Poor man. There is no place for him to go that will be good.

Thinking that about him, I know how lucky I am.

I've forgotten Little Dear, and now I remember.

A little ways off the freeway is a boarded-up house. Behind it, a dirt road snakes back into the trees. I follow the road and try to imagine that the house ever seemed new and that anybody ever lived in it. Then I am out of sight of the freeway and of the house, and I park beneath a tree. The sun comes down through the leaves and a stream gurgles close by. I close my eyes and listen to it, feeling suddenly warm, as if I've been cold and didn't know it.

Maybe this is what Eden was like, though I don't really believe there ever was an Eden.

I had a child when I was twenty. The father could have been either of two men, and neither of them ever knew that I was pregnant. Danny Boy was killed by a bee sting on the back porch of my parents' house where we lived when he was two. That was three years ago. Sometimes I try to remember how smooth his skin was. I know all kids are precious, but he looked more like an angel than the others. He slept with me and I used to love to listen to his heart and smell his breathing. At the funeral my mother told people over and over, "He hadn't done anything wrong yet. He was so little and he hadn't done anything wrong yet."

I met George right after that and I went to live with him in Atlanta. George cared a lot about me and said that he hoped someday I'd feel ready to have a child again. Then there was Jack. I saw his face first on a poster. It was black and white but his eyes stood out from it.   You could see how pale they were and you could imagine how nice it would be to have him really looking at you.   The poster announced that he was giving a reading.

We have good and bad ideas all the time and hardly ever know, when we have them, which they are.

I decided to go to the reading.

I'm not sure I believe that everything happens for a reason, but that could be true.   Maybe all this had to happen to really prepare George and me.

Maybe I had some kind of job in the world I needed to complete first.   Maybe killing Jack was my job.

Now that I've done it, if I can only get out from beneath the body, I can have my happily ever after.

I walk into the trees and squat to pee.

The long grass tickles the back of my thighs and my ass.   It rains on New Orleans and the wind blows and the people there feel what the people of Sodom and Gomorra must have felt like when the trembles before the crumbling began. It's not that they're worse in that city.   I suppose it's coming everywhere to everybody sometime or another.

There's a rustling sound, and I see that standing perfectly still off in the woods are two grubby looking boys, brothers, probably, with wild red hair.   The older one of them is wearing glasses and leering at me, his teeth yellow like the teeth of an old man.

I blink hard to make them go away, but they don't.

I'm still peeing and have to wait for it to stop before I can yell. "You get the hell out of here!"

The littlest one turns and scurries off, but the bigger one stands there. "We seen your bare ass!"   Then he lets out a sort of cackle.

I blink again.   When I open my eyes, he's almost gone, following the other one off into the woods.

I pull up my panties and stand, looking after the boys to see if they are really gone, and as far as I can tell, they are.

I walk down to where they stood and check for footprints, I suppose just to make sure that they really existed.

Decomposition

I sit down, tired, and let myself slump backward, until my spine is uncoiling against the ground. Between blinks, I see the blue sky, the green leaves. Then I don't see anything at all.

This is something close to sleep.

When I sit up, I'm worried. I look around right away and it takes me awhile to realize what I look for is the boys, and it takes me a little while longer yet to be sure they are not about.

Even then, I have the impression I've forgotten something, and so I continue to look around, feeling afraid despite the sun, all its warmth and light.

Then it comes to me: Little Dear.

I go back to the car and open the trunk. Little Dear looks up at me. Hanging from her beak is a bit of bloody skin and some whitish goop.

"What have you done?"

I look at Jack's face. One of his eyes is half pulled out of its socket and some of the eye itself it is gone. What is visible of the socket is bright red but not bloody. The eye is misshapen and the green of the iris and the black of the pupil seem to have been pulled into duplicate oblong shapes. A bubble of white oozes out from where Little Dear has pecked through the film.

I lift Little Dear out of the trunk. She gives a wet sounding cluck.

I can feel my fingers squeezing too hard against her body and I realize that I'm angry with her for what she's done to Jack. Then I think of all the things that I told her about how awful he was and how necessary his death.

I glance at him and away and then whisper to Little Dear, "You were doing that for me, weren't you?"

She makes a hard swallowing sound.

I relax my grip.

Now that I am calm, it is all right for me to face the fact that probably she wasn't performing an act of revenge against him. He's dead and he deserved that death and he deserves whatever Little Dear has done to him, but as for her, she was probably just hungry. Maybe she still is.

"Do you want more?"

I set her down close to Jack's face, and then I turn away. I hear her peck and I hear the sound of something pulled. I hear her cluck and swallow and peck again. I hear the sound of something stretched and then I hear a snap.

I was late for the reading. Jack was in the middle of answering questions. He looked so sure of himself and so handsome I could hardly stand it. We fucked that night. It was wild fucking, during which he squeezed my wrists and held my hands over my head and beat himself against me. I came hard. He took me with him to Savannah where he had another reading. I didn't tell George I was going.

Jack said, "You're a lovely girl. You have pretty eyes. But they don't look happy. You look like you're being wasted. You need a new place to be."

I went back to Atlanta and got my car and my things while George was at work. I never saw him again, but eventually he sent a long e-mail telling me that I had shattered him. He was leaving Atlanta. He wrote that he didn't know what had happened and that even if he did, he'd never be able to understand it, and that wherever I was, he couldn't wish me luck.

I know what I did to you was awful, George, but I'm going to make it up. I'm going to mend your heart and I'm going to let you be my all-time hero.

Before then, I have this, my adventure, my journey.

After that first trip to Savannah, Jack didn't take me to his readings or conferences, but I wasn't threatened by the idea that he was doing with some other girl what he'd done with me.

I think of Kimberly, the student of Jack's who moved in across the street from us. She's not nearly as good looking as I am. None of his students were. The only thing they had on me was that their pussies were new to him, and I suppose I believed that one day he'd get up the gumption to cheat. One of the reasons I did all of the strange things Jack wanted to do sexually was because I knew that was the way he was trying to keep me new.

I turn around and see there is nothing left of Jack's eye. Just the red socket and some goop in it.

"Come on," I tell Little Dear, feeling a little angry again, but not sure at whom.

She seems overly calm as I lift her out of the trunk. In the sunlight, I can see her beak has flakes of blood and flesh on it.

I'd forgotten I sprayed him, but now I can smell the insect repellent coming off of her.

I'm still tired and the air is warm and the stream gurgles, and it is time for us to move on.

We drive into the sun. Big and perfectly round, not like a ball of fire, but like a red glowing disc.

Little Dear has sunk down with her legs curled under her.

I want to stay awake. I suppose I want her to stay awake, too. I tell her that the world is not good and that it is not bad. I tell her the world is indifferent. I tell her that just the same, we will make our own goodness in it. She cocks her head and shudders.

And we drive into twilight.

And we drive past the point the sun has set and into the darkness, Little Dear and me, on a road that will eventually lead exactly where we need it to.

I grip something in a blackness, this sleep as dreamless as death. It is only the wheel in my hands that connects me to the world, and only just barely, like something I won't push away or pull close but mean to keep at arm's length.

I don't want to wake.

But I'm not sure about all this dark, either.

I want to summon big glass windows with sunshine coming through them, little birds on the rail outside, peace and ease. And it's there, a sheet of glass brightly lit, and I know I have a face only because I feel myself smile.

The surface beneath me changes. At first I bump along and then I feel as if I'm sliding. I want to understand, but I don't think I will.

I open my eyes.

Headlights cut through long grass.

I hear a long and loud wail. The horn of a truck. I stomp on the brake pedal.

The car slides and slides and then finally stops with a jerk. My breasts flatten against the steering wheel. Little Dear flops onto the floor.

After a moment, I hear Jack falling back into place in the trunk.

When I can move, I leap out of the car as if it's still dangerous to be inside.

The ground is mushy, the car slightly sunken.

What I feel like is a princess in an unfamiliar place, some King's daughter who got to that point in the story where you think she really might not make it.

What I tell myself is that it's not as bad as all that.

What I tell myself is the truth: I've fallen asleep at the wheel and have skidded into the median and there is nothing really to worry about. People do this kind of thing every day.

I look for the truck that honked. There will be some kind-faced man in his middle ages, a man who looks like a woodcutter, one of those forest people from a fairy tale who knows he was put on earth to help people. He'll carry me and Little Dear out of this mess, and then he'll pull free the Mustang so that we can get back on our way.

But the truck's not slowing. Only the red lights show and soon they are gone.

And I know that was just a truck driver and not some hero.

What I'm telling myself is that that is OK. What I suggest to myself is that probably I can get out of this on my own.

Jack's face glows in the trunk light. The hole into his head where his eye was seems especially red.

"Jack?"

I want him to calm him.

I want him to help me.

I want to know he's OK.

And I know none of these are good wants.

And when I reach in, I know that need to touch is not good either. He is cold, and his hair, as I try to smooth it, feels brittle.

I stroke his head until I feel at ease, and then I continue to touch him until I feel numb. I stroke him past that, until I am fully aware that he is dead and it is his corpse I touch.

Going through the entire process like that makes me feel sane.

I tell myself I was prepared for the trip to be this complicated. That when I set all this in motion I had weighed out the costs against what I would gain. That there was a choice to be made and I made it.

"I killed you for a reason," I say.

But I can't quit touching him. Maybe I'd never stop, if a voice didn't say, "Ma'am?"

I turn around. There is a middle-aged man in a flannel shirt and a baseball cap. Behind him is a small pickup truck, pulled off the side of the freeway.

"Are you all right?"

I take my hand off Jack. Without turning away from the man, I close the trunk.

"Ma'am?"

"Yes."

"You're all right?"

He comes closer to me. I think his face is kind, but it is hard to read his eyes beneath the bill of his cap. Maybe there are a few fairy tale heroes after all. But what comes off of him is the smell of fast food French fries. I have the sudden need to throw up.

I cover my mouth with my hand and I say, as best as I can, "I think I'm stuck."

"What happened—did you fall asleep?"

"Yes."

"You got to find a hotel. You can't just drive when you're tired."

"I know."

"What were you getting out of the trunk?" His head tilts and I see the flash of the white of his eye. It looks all knowing, like the kind of eye that doesn't even need to see a body in a trunk to know it's there. He doesn't look like a savior anymore, but like a judge of some kind, the person who slowly and calmly pronounces an end to your adventure.

"Will you push me?"

"Yes."

He has gotten closer and the smell of French fries is so strong my stomach convulses. It's not just that I don't want to throw up in front of the man. It's that I don't want to throw up at all. I didn't do it when I killed Jack, so why should I do it now?

I step away and turn and start down the side of the car.

Little Dear lies in a disheveled heap on the floor. I pick her up and put her back on the seat. Her head droops.

"You're tired, too," I say.

I turn on the car, and it occurs to me there is only one thing to do. I look in the rear view mirror. The man is all red in the taillights, and that makes him look not like a real man at all. I watch as in reflection he leans forward and puts his hands on the trunk, and I realize that I can do what I have to do. I tell myself I have to run him over for the sake of me and Little Dear. I tell myself that George will suffer a life of loneliness if I don't finish this journey.

I do it for all of us, me and George and Little Dear. In war you choose the side of yourself and those you love, even though you understand that the people against you think they're just as right.

This man, he's my enemy, whether he meant to be or not.

I roll down the window.

"Thanks," I say.

"Go," the man says.

I shift into reverse, still watching in the rear view mirror. The red lights become brighter and the man looks up with a surprised expression. I step on the gas. The wheels spin and then catch.

"Wait!" The man yells and dives sideways, and the car spins backward, jerking and bumping around so it's hard to say whether or not I've hit and run over him.

I brake and shift quickly into the drive gear. I step on the gas again. The car swings around and then the tires catch and we go skittering through the grass and up onto the interstate.

I still don't look back. I never will.

This motel—two stories high, long and flat with small windows covered in heavy looking curtains—it's the kind of place salesmen stop to kill themselves. Trashy people meet to fuck behind the backs of other trashy people.

We could just keep going, but no one can do that forever.

"It's all right," I tell Little Dear. "We'll be fine."

There's no house on a hill behind the motel. No dead old lady in the window. There's not even a hill.

"It's really just fine," I say.

Little Dear looks at me skeptically, but it's just the light that makes her seem like that. It's just my state of mind.

It's important for me to know what's real from what I project.

It's important to be honest with myself, because if I allow myself too many illusions, I won't make this journey.

The truth is, not only is Little Dear not looking at me skeptically, she's not looking at me at all.

And I tell myself that's all right. She doesn't have to understand every word I say. She doesn't have to look at me all the time.

As I park and get out, I think about how they have ferries out of Seattle. Maybe George and I will take one to Vancouver, that city on the island you hear about, and we'll stay in a high-rise hotel and look down from our huge windows at all the lights and the sea beyond them.

How beautiful that will be, and all of this, behind me, will be worth it.

There's a teenage boy as receptionist, and I feel his eyes on me as I fill out the paperwork. I suppose he knows he'll never have a girl like me. I want to tell him that that is all right, and that he will eventually have somebody—most everybody does—and that when he does, he ought to be happy with her. I want to tell him that he should make certain she knows that he is happy, because when you don't believe you're making your lover happy, you yourself cannot be.

Really, if he can just understand and accept these things, he'll be all right.

I look up, ready to tell him some or all of this. His eyebrows are shaggy and he's got pimples on his cheeks and his upper lip is cracked. I can't help but feel disgusted.

I take the paperwork a few steps away from the counter to finish filling it out.

Jack gave me this credit card with my name on it. He was always good about giving me things. My father was that way, too. For everything that was wrong, he could figure out something to give me. When Danny Boy died was the only time it didn't seem like he could think of a thing. I use Jack's card now, and after the boy has swiped it and waited for a few moments, he hands it back to me and smiles.

I'm surprised by how even and white his teeth are.

Staring at his mouth, I forget about all the things wrong with his face, and I almost forget that he'll never know what it is like to dance with a beautiful woman or to kiss one or to go beyond that, that he'll never know what it is like to put his hand in her panties, his penis in her vagina.

"You'll be all right," I tell him.

"Miss?"

It's all right. I don't need to make him know what I mean.

The room is large enough. It has two beds, each with a red comforter. There is a small TV locked on top of a stand, and there is a desk and a dresser. I put Little Dear on one of the beds. She's been very quiet. Right away, she puts her head down and to the side. I move to lift it up again but then decide to just let her be.

Without undressing, I lay down on the other bed.

Something smells. Maybe it's me. I'm not going to shower, though. I'm not going to do anything.

Killing Jack and lugging the body into the garage and getting him into the trunk of the car and freeing Little Dear and driving all day and then getting the car stuck and trying to run the Samaritan over, it's all just sapped me.

It's all I can do to reach over and turn out the light.

"Goodnight," I say to Little Dear.

She doesn't cluck.

Or move.

But I know she's alive.

In this kind of story, something doesn't just die on you.

It's almost always hard to sleep. And unless I've come, it's pretty much impossible. Jack believed in rituals. He told me that having an orgasm before drifting off was one of mine. At first, he liked it. Later, he didn't.

My hand has gone up my dress without my even thinking about it. My fingers roll around, but nothing is going to happen unless I think of something, so I try to think of George.

I try, but I just can't. I can't get his picture in my head for more than a flash, and when I do, I don't feel turned on.

So naturally, Jack shows up. He stands there with his swollen cock. No matter what kind of selfish asshole he was, his prick was beautiful. I'm fingering myself and thinking about Jack and I've got to stop. I've got to get him out of this fantasy. I've got to get him out my mind in general.

I go back to George but the thought of him causes my fingers to still.

Then I try the homosexual cop. In my fantasy he is pushing my legs open and looking at my pussy. It's the first one he's seen. He looks up at my face. His is vulnerable; I can see that he is overwhelmed but compelled. He pushes his head forward and begins licking and nibbling me with a hunger he never knew he had in him.

Just as I'm about to come, Little Dear makes a strange noise, like a release of air.

I sit up and turn on the light. She is on her side, though her head is lifted and cocked. Her legs are splayed out strangely. Her beak is open. I can see her little gray tongue.

"What's the matter?"

She just stays like that.

She hardly drank any water today and I think maybe that is it. I go to the bathroom and put water in the plastic cup and bring it back and hold it before her. She seems to look at it and then she lays her head back on the bed. She must be tired too, but she doesn't look like she's trying to sleep.

"You'll feel better tomorrow," I tell her.

I put the cup on the table and turn off the light. Then I lie down and try to go to sleep without coming. Little Dear is making noises and I can't quit thinking about her. I wonder if she's ever been fucked. I've seen that before. The rooster holds the chicken by the back of the neck and bends his tail to hers. I couldn't really tell if there is a penis. I couldn't really tell if there is anything about it she likes.

Little Dear makes another sound. It's like a gasp. I get up and turn on the light again. Little Dear is trying to rise. A bloody looking stream of shit spurts out from beneath her tail feathers. The stink of it is awful. She begins beating her wings and letting out a cackling sound. It's all very ugly. There's an urge I have to pick her up and wring her neck so that we can both be finished with it.

But I don't do that.

"It's going to be OK," I say. I pat her head. She jerks it away and shits more. Then she lifts her head straight up and makes another cackling sound. She looks at me with her mouth open, as if she wants to tell me something. Her wings beat again and then still. Her head falls. She breathes heavily and then she doesn't breathe.

When I am sure she is dead, I wash her off under the bathtub faucet. Then I wrap her in one of the white towels. Little Dear, all bundled up. Nothing has looked cleaner.

I could wait until tomorrow, but I feel I must bury her now. There are so many things you have to get behind you.

The teenager is still sitting there with his pimples and his shaggy eyebrows and his misplaced, pretty teeth. I don't want to ask him for a shovel.

On one end of the walk that goes in front of all the second floor rooms there is a little door. That it is locked convinces me that what I want is inside. I just lift up my foot and kick. Something gives. I do it again and hear wood splinter.

I look around. No lights have come on. No room doors have opened.

I cock my foot, feeling the muscles of my thighs and ass constrict, feeling powerful, the same way I felt the first time I hit Jack. That was after I showed him a sketch I'd made of him. He stared at it for a few moments and then giggled. Before I thought about anything, I closed my hand and hit him in the side of the head. His grin fell, and I was ready for him to hit me back, but he didn't. He took hold of me and pulled me against him and wouldn't let go. He swayed back and forth with me and said over and over that he was sorry.

This was different than the way he held me most of the time. I could really feel him. And against him, I could really feel myself.

I kick again, as hard as I can, and the door gives further.

It makes me sad to think about the good times we had and whatever bit of love he really felt for me.

But he's dead and that's his fault and regret will be of no use to either of us now.

I kick one more time and the door swings open.

I go in. As my eyes adjust to the deeper darkness within, I make out open boxes with toilet paper and things like that in them. There is one of those carts the housekeeping people push around.

The best thing I can find to dig with is a dustpan. It will do.

I go downstairs and get Little Dear and take her and the dustpan out into the field behind the motel. There I begin scooping up earth and little bits of rocks. A few inches down, it gets harder. Soon I have to cut up the earth with the tip of the dustpan and then scoop out what I've cut up. It takes a long time to get even as deep as she is, and to bury her like that is to not really bury her at all.

I look at the motel and think about just walking back there, leaving Little Dear as she is. This wouldn't make a difference, not really, not to anybody, not even her.

But I can't do it. So I guess that means it does make a difference to me.

Off to the side of the field there is a forest, and in it I break a branch off a tree. One end is now jagged, and I use it to hack up the earth so that I can dig it out with my hands and the dust-pan. After a while, I have a decent enough hole.

I put her in it.

It's really very simple.

I look up at the stars and back down at the hole and the towel in there and I know that she is all wrapped up in that towel.

I could cry for Little Dear, which might be cleansing, but I don't want to do that. I am afraid any little flow might open me up and I don't want to start sobbing, the same way I didn't want to throw up.

There are just times when you've got to hold stuff inside yourself.

Later, I can cry. Or throw up. But when this trip is over, why would I want to?

I could tell myself she is just a chicken. Just a creature I hardly knew. We can say that about anybody, about anything, and sometimes, you need to. Sometimes saying that is good enough.

I begin to scoop the dirt back in. When the hole is filled and I've built a little mound, I stomp down on it. Everything gives a little bit and I'm aware for a moment that I'm crushing her, but this is what we do with the dead.

Some fairy tales really are grim. I tell this to myself as I walk back toward my room.

I tell myself that I suppose it was one of those stories where some precious thing has been kept so long in the darkness that when it is finally rescued and exposed to light, it dies.

I am sorry she is dead, but I can't let it make me lose hope. Everything dies, but I have not died. There is still a chance for me. I might still get to be that girl my mother told me about, that pretty housewife with the husband who comes happily through the door, whose children go off happily to school, whose dog plays happily in the yard, that girl who goes on wonderful vacations twice a year, once with both her husband and kids, and once with just her husband so that they can pretend they are strangers and fuck like they did when they barely knew each other.

I am ready to be that girl.

I'm at the car and I'm not going to make any excuses about what I'm doing. There are no good reasons for me to open the trunk, but I open it anyway. It's been about twenty hours. Jack's still stiff with *rigor mortis* and there is a feint odor to him.

I want to look at his prick.

I pretend that I just wonder if death has stiffened it into a hard-on. In honesty, I just need to see his cock. We fucked less and less the longer we knew each other; but even if they became few and far in between and were difficult to get out of him, every fuck with Jack was good.

I open the sheets more. His knees won't unfold and his waist won't untwist. I struggle to get his pajama pants down but can't do so without totally repositioning him. Finally, I just reach in. His skin is cold. I find his dick. It is not hard. It doesn't fill my hand, doesn't seem like so much now. I can feel my eyes squeezing closed and then seeping open, but the blackness I see starts before I blink and lasts afterward.

And then there is Jack's dick in my hand. It will never fill with blood again, never stir, rise up, never penetrate anything.

I let it go; there's nothing else to do.

I close the trunk; there's nothing else to do.

I wash my hands over and over, like Lady Macbeth.

Then I wash my face.

Nothing seems enough.

I put on my moisturizer. I pluck my eyebrows. I look at my face for a long time. It's not supposed to look good now. Nobody always looks good.

My sundress is filthy. I take it off and put it in the wastepaper basket. I brought one other, a sundress too. That's what Jack liked me to wear and he bought both of these. I'm supposed to be free of his ideas, but I looked good in sundresses before Jack knew me and I look good in them now that he is not here to know me.

So I'm a little dirty. So I'm little tired. So my traveling companion is dead and buried. So my dead boyfriend is in the trunk of my car when he should be buried. So what to all of these things: I look at myself in the mirror in the fresh sundress that shows my legs and accentuates my waist and bosom, and I look good again.

I know this trip is going to be hard, but I'll get there. I don't even know where George is, exactly, but I'll find him.

My father told me that there are people in the world who see an obstacle as a reason to give up and those that see an obstacle as proof that what they want really is on the other side. I must be one of those people. This is my story and I'm going to get to the happy ending.

I could try to sleep, but it wouldn't work. I'll just go now, just get into my car and drive.

North and west. The way is clear.

This is that darkness before dawn. I know that.

This is as alone as I've been, but the gas station opens at five. I know that, too.

This is not a dream and the world is not dead.

I know that.

I keep telling myself these things. That the sun will rise. And it will. That the day will warm. And it will. That everything will be fine. And it will.

Day II.

It's hard to imagine there was ever water here. All I see is dust and rock, this worn out riverbed that looks like it could never have held river.

What state I'm in doesn't matter.

I am on this bridge in the sun. Dried out grass extends from the edge of the riverbed, and beyond that, a forest just goes on and on.

Jack's been dead about thirty hours.

Imagine him standing here, in this wind, with all this prettiness around. Maybe he'd be inspired to write something. If I had real art in me, I'd want to sketch this place. I'd want to sketch myself in it. That kind of thing, though, the ability to create, that's what Jack did. Or at least what he was supposed to be doing. Me, I just had these silly sketches. I knew they weren't good even before he giggled that time I showed him one.

And maybe he didn't do them often enough, but Jack was capable of romantic acts. It is possible to imagine the two of us fleeing the hurricane together and stopping here to sit on the edge of the bridge with our legs dangling over. He'd take my hand and we'd run down the embankment and off into the woods. Eventually, we'd roll together in the leaves and the grass. It is possible to imagine us like that, on a day like this, pressed together as if we were meant to live a happily ever after.

This is what they always told you it would be like, all those songs and love movies.

We'd fuck, beautiful in this light.

Imagine this lovely couple, fucking out there, and climbing back up onto the bridge afterwards. Imagine them standing at the edge, arms outstretched, hands touching. Then they leap. Jack and me, soaring into our deaths, the ultimate act of lovers.

It's all so romantic it brings tears to my eyes.

I'm not going to cry. I'm not going to think of Jack like that. I'm going to remember that the nice thing about George is you'd never think about dying with him. George, there is a man you can live with.

Jack, he collected books, and he was always telling me to read one of them or another. After I would read it, he would ask me to talk about it. He'd sit there looking at me as if he couldn't believe the book hadn't fixed what was he thought was wrong with me.

He wasn't so smart, anyway. Jack just wanted people to think he read more than he did. Before we'd have a visitor, he'd take books off the shelves and scatter them around, open-spined, as if they were being read. What he wanted was for people to walk up and down his shelves reading titles and assuming that it was all a reflection of his inner-self, as if since he'd collected them all, the stories and ideas in all those books were somehow his.

But whatever he thought about them, whatever he thought they were doing for him, it's all gone now.

We're not going to fuck and leap. We were never going to do anything like that, Jack. Your brain is just a blob of pink and gray meat, still and empty, and nothing—nothing at all—can make it think again.

It will rot like the rest of you.

Below are leaves and rocks and dirt, and I could bury him easily enough there. He'd turn to dust and disappear.

What would be left of him then would only be left in my mind.

Couldn't I clean it then?

I ought to want to do that.

He was a phony. He was small. He was. But damn it, I keep on wanting him to rise up out of the trunk and stand beside me anyway.

If I can't get him behind me, there is no point in going forward.

I think like this and find myself climbing up onto the railing. At first, I'm not alone. He's standing right with me. When I die in the dust down there, I will settle with him. Maybe we can be romantic like that after all.

But then I see myself from the outside, beautiful, with the sky light blue above me, the wind in my hair. He's not beside me. I am free, and when I jump, it will be alone, and this feels like the strongest moment I've ever had.

I close my eyes and point my toes, the way you do on a diving board.

Then George does exactly what he is supposed to, exactly what he would in a movie or a song.

He saves me from my strength.

He says, "I'm waiting."

George and I will never fuck in the leaves and grass, but I know that what he said is true. I know that he's waiting. That's reason enough to go on.

And I get down.

Then it gets better.

George says, "Just say 'fuck you.'"

D composition

I've never actually heard him say "fuck" before.

"Tell him," George says.

"Fuck you, Jack," I say.

And I get in the car.

I order two biscuits and coffee at a diner attached to the gas station where I've filled up. I eat and drink without real hunger or thirst.

A guy at the counter, he's eating chicken, but I'm not going to get sentimental.

I ask the waitress how to get to the nearest interstate, and she explains. I know I probably shouldn't, but I tell her I'm going to Seattle.

I say, "It's very lovely there."

She says she wouldn't know.

I say, "It's not like New Orleans." She arches her eyebrows and makes as if to pat my hand but then doesn't.

I say, "Or Atlanta. Or any place I've ever been."

This waitress is probably fifty, thin with a bad dye job and gaudy makeup. She stands there with her coffee pot and looks down at me and what I see is her sadness. I see the way she is trapped and always has been. Her skin is blotchy and her bluish waitress outfit makes her hips look huge. She could be pretty if she knew how. I wish I were her daughter, as if I could make things all right for her then. Like one of those girls on a talk show, "I'd say, 'I love you, Ma, but you really got to get with it.'" Then there would be a makeover and when she saw herself afterwards, she'd feel fulfilled in a way she's never been before. We'd go off together, this little team, this perfect bond, something I never knew.

I tip her well.

It's the best real thing I can do for her.

From what I learned about decomposition, Jack shouldn't stink yet. But he must, because the car does.

Maybe the night was hot.

Maybe being in the trunk of a car speeds up the process.

Maybe it's something rotten in Jack that makes him go bad faster.

Or, maybe, it is just in my mind.

I'm not going to pretend a mind doesn't trick a person, especially when it's sleepy. I've got to remember to allow for this and think about everything carefully.

Wherever the smell comes from, it gets stronger as I follow the waitress's instructions down a series of roads to the interstate. There I join the flow of traffic and the wind whips in through the open windows. Still, I can smell something that I assume to be rot, and it's getting worse.

I hope it is just my imagination.

In truth, I don't like to think of Jack decaying.

There is the blue Wal-Mart sign, standing up on two off-white pillars.

My mother did not shop at Wal-Mart or allow that anyone in her family would. At least once a week, usually on Saturday, my father and I would drive to the one close to our house and wander around anyway. This was our main secret. We'd buy candy and eat it in the shade of the wall outside.

Depending on what time zone I am in, it is a little after twelve or one. People are here in droves, just as they always were at the Wal-Mart my father and I went to. I park and get out. But then I just stand there, thinking that in some ways I've turned out like my mother, because the idea of going in amongst the kind of people that I know are inside Wal-Mart disgusts me just as it does her.

She wasn't wrong about everything she told me.

Nobody is.

Just like Jack wasn't all bad.

The store is crowded. These are the people my mother hates. Maybe it comes from fear, of their fatness, their ugliness, the way they are too easily pleased by junk. I don't want anybody here to touch me, not even by accident, and so I walk with my hands up by my shoulders, my eyes narrowed to focus a path in front of me the way you do in an emergency.

A face emerges from all the faces, an unshaven chin, unshaven cheeks, marked red beneath the bristles, eyes leering, nose pointed, the whole thing aimed at me.   I sidestep, into a woman, not her as a whole, necessarily, but her bosom, that kind you associate with kindergarten teachers, and I yelp, spin, turn, spin again, past faces and rolls of flesh beneath and coming out of cheap clothing. I start to run, hands up high, tummy sucked in, trying to make myself small.

Then I am standing alone in an aisle full of body care products; I pick up a two pack of Baby Fresh deodorant.   I make it quickly to a self check out and wait my turn, standing back a bit. I've done this to avoid dealing with a cashier, but the items won't scan, and so a little fat woman comes over anyway.

The Mustang is safety.

Just me, just Jack.

I drive out of the crowded lot and down the road until I find what looks like private place behind a large brick building.

There, I open the trunk, the stale smell not as bad as I expected.

I've forgotten about Jack's eye, and the hole stands out red and black.   I immediately look at the other eye, but that's not much better.   It's as if that eye is made of glass.   Or as if it's just a picture of an eye.

I look away.

I tell myself I will not look at the missing or remaining eye. I tell myself I'm done with his eyes.

I open the sheet.   He's not as stiff as he was before.   The *rigor mortis* must be in its last stage.   I spread apart his bathrobe so that the muscles of his chest and stomach are visible.

There's grayness to his skin; I don't like that.

But I've killed him; this is how it is supposed to be.

I yank the shoulders of his bathrobe down toward his elbows. More gray skin. In the cramp of the trunk, it's hard to maneuver this stick of chemical smelling baby powder around Jack's stiff torso.   Chunks of the deodorant break off and I leave a lump of it between his shoulder blades, thinking he'll never feel it, like that story of the princess and the pea.   Or maybe—I can't remember—she did feel it. Anyway, I deodorize his armpits and then the bottoms of his feet. Then I open the second stick. I can't get his pajama bottoms down so I just thrust my hand down there and smear deodorant all around, up and down his thighs and down the crack of his ass as much as I can with the cheeks clenched up as they are, around his cock and balls and the whole pubic area. When I bring it out, the stick's got little hairs all over it.

Jack was the kind of slob who once he believed he didn't have to earn your respect anymore, you could see so by the whiskers he'd leave in the tub and the way that it got grimy in there. After he'd bathed, there'd be a ball of hair in the drain. He was losing it off the top of his head and trying to hide that from everybody. If I'd accidentally get above him and see it, I'd close my eyes and turn away.

At least he doesn't smell so bad anymore. But I stink. I wipe the deodorant pubic hairs off on Jack's chest, and then I apply the deodorant to my own underarms.

Now all I can smell is baby powder, which I should have re-membered is not really a good smell, not after you've had a baby, anyway, when you'll associate the smell with shit. Not when your baby is long dead and what you really think about when you smell it is that.

Here is Jack folded up and half stiff before me, with one gone and one eye dead. Here he is starting to stink. What I am is repulsed, and this gives me strength. If I were in the proper place, I think I could go with my disgust and just roll his body out and get on with my trip, but this is not a proper place.

I pull up Jack's pajama bottoms and close his bathrobe and fold the sheet back over him.

Lid closed.

Job done.

I need clothes.

Some people, they get into an emergency and just let them-selves go. Not me.

Down the street is a Ross's Dress-for-Less in a strip mall. Right next door is an Old Navy, but I'd never wear their stuff, not any more than I'd wear stuff bought from Wal-Mart or Target. Ross's sells name brands, just discounted, and there is nothing wrong with that.

Jack liked to come clothes shopping with me. He was the opposite of George in that he had advice for me on almost anything, what I ate, what I wore, how I talked. It was too much, as if Jack wanted to be in absolute control of me. With George, it was too little, as if since he didn't care about any of those things you had to wonder if really cared at all.

Jack, he'd say, "Freedom is chaos."

And George, well George never said very much.

When Jack told you that you were beautiful, you knew he meant it, that he'd really looked at you and held you up against other women he'd seen. George would say it, too, but because you thought he'd say it no matter what, it didn't mean much.

Anyway, what I need to do is choose something that will make George take note. This outfit, it has to be perfect. It has to say so many things.

It has to say that I really am beautiful, and not just to him.

It has to say that I'm untarnished.

It has to say that I'm sorry.

And it has to say that I'm truly ready.

I go to the bathroom to check myself.

I can't really like what I see, but that's to be expected this far into a journey. I wash my face and hands. I wash around my neck and I reach up my dress and wash around my vagina. I apply a little lipstick and eyeliner. I don't look so bad. My hair is sort of out of control and so I tie it back; then it looks all right. Now nobody can guess by looking at me all the things I've done and been through in the last thirty-five hours. I smile and give myself a wink and touch up my lipstick one more time.

As I walk into the store, I realize that this is the best I've looked in a long time.

I wander around, waiting for something to catch my eye. It is not long before I notice a woman watching me. She's tall and blond and has a cute nose and cheek bones that stand out enough to get your attention, but not so much that you feel like you're looking at her skull. She's got a narrow waist and well rounded boobs and on top of all this, she is very well dressed. She glances away from me and then back again.

Right away I know what she is doing: she's the other hot woman in here, and so she's sizing me up to see which of us looks best.

Even though I'm at a complete disadvantage after everything I've been through, I want to know, too. The way that gunfighters are supposed to always have a need to find out who was the fastest.

She looks away again and takes the sleeve of a jacket between two of her fingers. I step behind a rack of jeans and walk quickly down the aisle and then circle around so I can come up behind her. She is standing to the side and looking toward the place I've just been. Her breasts, standing out like that, so big on her little frame, are probably fake.

My breasts are, and I'm not ashamed of that.

Jack bought them with money he won for an award for his novel. My natural breasts were nice, but Jack talked about seeing a plastic surgeon for a few months, and by the time we were sitting in the doctor's office, it felt like it had been my idea. Anyway, I appreciated that he was making an investment in me. I took it as a compliment that he was trying to perfect me.

At first, I dreamt sometimes that I had died and decomposed but the breasts did not, my skeleton there in its coffin with these mounds still standing up off of it, the skin all peeled away and the plastic showing through.

After a while, I got used to them, and even though they don't totally refocus Jack on me, they seemed to help for a month or two. They're mine now, as much as any other part of me. Though they are bigger than the other woman's breasts, her frame is slighter than mine, so I guess you might have to call it a tie.

I pretend to look at some panties and work my way down the rack so that I can get off to her side and really study her profile. She has yet to spot me, and I think I've got a good two or three seconds. Her chin is strong and her nose really is perfect. Of her skin I'm not certain, but it has an even color and an appearance of clarity. She turns to me full on. Instead of looking away,

I go ahead and study the rest of her face for anything that throws it off the balance. There is a slight discolorization just under her eye, but I bet people call that a beauty mark, even though it faults her symmetry.

She's studying my face, too. Her eyes are blue and clear and look not unlike my own. She breaks first, looking away. I don't know if this means she has decided she is hotter than I am or just the opposite, if she is satisfied or humiliated.

As she turns and starts down the aisle, I look at her ass. I know what men like: asses that stand out. Hers is small and flat. I do specific exercises in the gym just to give my ass lift. Even as most of his compliments died out, Jack would still comment on my ass. George never said anything about it, but I'm sure that in his silence he liked it, too. I'm sure he'll like it again, even though he might not be able to say it. He couldn't talk to me in the way that Jack did about things like that; just the word "vagina" would make him blush and cough into his hand. That's all right. I'll teach George how to say, "Nice ass." I'll teach him it's okay to talk about my pussy sometimes.

Well, maybe I'll teach him those things.

Maybe, though, it doesn't matter if he can talk like that or not. Maybe it shouldn't matter. Maybe I should teach myself not to like to hear those words coming out of a man's mouth.

Anyway, the flatness of this woman's ass cinches it for me. I turn away, feeling satisfied, until I catch my own reflection in a mirror at the end of a rack. Lipstick is coming off the corner of my lip and an inch onto my cheek, a red mark that looks like a cut.

I blush, even though I know this smear doesn't really make me less or more beautiful in the long run.

The contest is invalidated.

For this kind of duel to work, the flat assed woman and I should be stripped naked and washed completely free of makeup and made to stand in bright light. Then we'd see.

I'd stand up well, then.

I'd be the real winner, then.

I've had a baby, but I'm unmarred.

The woman who Jack had me fuck had a series of rivets and waves on her belly, like a sheet that had been slept on. She had had two children. When I came back home and admitted I was pregnant, my mother spread a cream on my belly and thighs every night, gritting her teeth and telling me it would keep me smooth, her fingers digging in sometimes as if she was having a hard time keeping herself from hurting me. Now I've got only the smallest dimple of a mark on my belly, just below the button. It is hard to see and doesn't necessarily make me look like I've had a baby—it doesn't really seem to prove Danny Boy existed or is gone.

A little mark, it could be anything, any type of scar.

It wouldn't put me beneath this woman. Still, I know that because of the lipstick she has satisfied herself that she is the queen of this room.

Fair or unfair, I've lost, and there is nothing I can do about it.

I go back to the car and have to stifle the urge to open the trunk and look at Jack, as if he could make me feel completely beautiful now even though he for a long time failed to do that when he was alive.

I don't want to see his dead eye and missing eye anyway.

I'm going to have to do something about that.

I get in the car. I'll buy clothes sometime later. And I'll check my makeup well before I go into that store, and when I do, I will be like a beam of light under which everyone else will wither.

Seek seek seek.

Wanting badly for some song to capture me, I push the button so many times I'm wearing a little divot of soreness into the tip of my finger. I'm waiting for a beat and some words I can't ignore, a song that will fill me with magic and lift me up, the soundtrack for this trip.

The truth is, I feel lonely.

And all the songs are bad memory songs or songs that just don't inspire me or some radio add that sounds like every other radio add or some radio host that sounds like every other host.

I could really use something special right now.

decomposition

I'm sort of sad about a couple of things. For one, I'm really completely done with Wal-Marts. It's strange: all those visits when with my father when I was a child, and I became like my mother about that anyway.

And it's definitely sad to me that Jack is starting to stink. I wish this was the kind of world where once something died, it just disappeared. No rot. No smell. No skeleton. No ashes to ashes and all that. But it's not that kind of world, and here I am lugging Jack's body around.

What it all boils down to, I think, what I'm sad about, is that I'm losing things. This is good and bad and most certainly necessary.

I wish there was somebody to tell me a story.

Jack liked to watch movies. At least once a week he'd pick up a DVD at the store down the street and I'd fall asleep while we watched it and wake up with him still watching.

"You missed it," he'd say, and kiss me. "Don't worry. Go back to sleep."

I never said there weren't good times. If it weren't for the good times, none of this would have been necessary. And if it was only good times, and if there was only good in him, then none of this would have been necessary. But that isn't true either. The truth is, down inside of him, there was something wrong with Jack.

There was something small and dirty.

Jack shrunk in front of me as he pumped his dirt into me. I had to kill him to rescue myself. I had to kill him to be free of him.

I can smell him.

If I braked hard, I'd hear him roll around in there.

I wish I were free, but I'm not, and the only thing I've got going for me is that I know it.

He's got two eyes. The one that is missing and the one that is dead. I know I'm not supposed to look at them anymore, but I can't help seeing them in my mind. I can't help knowing that I'm going to look for real at least one more time. There is no way to mend what's happened to his eyes, but I can't help needing it mended.

There are signs every few yards telling me to stop and see the largest collection of erotic DVDs in the nation, telling me that up ahead are the cheapest adult tapes anywhere, that I'm about to miss the widest variety of adult magazines I've ever seen, signs telling me that in the middle of this nowhere is the greatest porn shop in the world.

There are also signs that tell me about Jesus and salvation. Signs that tell me about the shame of abortion and fornication and my sinner's heart.

Blessed are the meek, says one.

XXX Super Sale! says another.

CHRIST DIED FOR YOUR SINS, says one.

Adult Toy Blowout! says another.

All I know is that I will get Jack eyes.

I pull off the interstate and park in front of the large squat square of logs, my car one amongst many vehicles in the football field sized lot, none of them close to another, as if they are all ashamed and wanted to be parked alone.

On the other side of the interstate is a church, white and pointing, like a finger, to God.

Jack thought I didn't understand anything about his world, but I know what the church and the porn shop facing each other across the interstate is: some kind of metaphor.

Inside, everything is brightly lit. There is a huge square of a glass counter full of dildos and handcuffs and lubricants and everything you've ever seen in a dirty movie or magazine. A plump little man stands behind a cash register inside that square. About a dozen other men wander around, and there are a few couples. I look nobody in the face.

The walls are lined with tapes and DVDs and magazines. It's all familiar enough.   I hadn't been in New Orleans for more than a month before Jack wanted to look at porno pictures and watch porno videos on the Internet while I sucked him off. Women getting fucked by many men.   Women fucking other women.   Close ups of tongues on cocks and tongues on clits and hands spreading ass cheeks and fingers going into holes. Cocks puffed about above cock rings and pussies dripping come.

It puts a strange feeling in my stomach to think about it now, Jack and I and all that stuff, but I will not say that looking at pictures like that is wrong. Sometimes, I liked them.

Right now, even, a little part of me still does.

Jack would thrust his cock in and out of my mouth while keeping his hand on the mouse, clicking through images. I'd look up and see his eyes slit and focused on the screen and no matter how good his cock felt at that time, I'd instantly hate him.

Sure, it didn't feel like hate then, but it feels like it now.

He took digital pictures and video tapes of me. He'd bring out skirts and panties and lingerie. Then he'd dress me and he would tell me to pose me this way and that way. "Sink your belly toward the floor. Raise your ass."

He'd bark out orders.

And he'd always get impatient, and sometimes he'd take pictures for so long there wouldn't really be much fuck left in him by the time we got to that. He was anxious to take the camera to his laptop and start looking through the pictures, trying to figure out which ones he should keep. Watching him do this, I always had the impression nothing ever looked quite like what he wanted it to.

I liked it better when he taped us fucking. He'd set up the camera and hook it to the television so we could watch ourselves on it. After a while he'd get the camera and zoom in on my cunt and his cock going into it, and he'd video me sucking him off. When the camera was on, he seemed more into it than he did when the camera was off.

What I wanted to think was that those pictures and those videos were things he would masturbate over when he was alone. When I asked him if that were true, he shrugged and said that he just liked having them. As if it was the idea of possessing he liked and not really the specific thing he possessed.

I wonder where they are now, all those images.

It doesn't matter. Those are pictures of who I once was, not who I am, and I am glad that I didn't think to try to take them with me.

I go to the gay section, where there will be men on the covers of the boxes.

There's a thin man in a green jacket there but he leaves immediately when I enter. I need a face that is about actual size, and I need eyes the greenish color of Jack's. Most of the faces are too small, or only one eye is showing, or the man has got a cock lifted to his mouth and I don't want the eyes from a picture like that.

Finally, there is a box that has a close up of a face that is nothing like Jack's. It is too young and the hair is too blond. But the eyes are the right size and a close enough color. I take this to the counter.

"I need scissors," I tell the man.

"I don't sell scissors," he says.

"Okay. Tape?"

"Like Scotch tape?"

"Yes, please."

He seems to think for a moment. Then he says, "Tape I can do."

I buy the video and he gives me a roll of tape. I look for the man in the green shirt so that I can give him the cassette, but he's nowhere to be seen, so I just take it out of the box and leave it on the counter.

I feel sort of sad leaving the store, like this is the last time I'll ever be in something like it.

I tear the eyes out of the box and then fold back the white flecks of cardboard all around the edges.

They look a little ragged, but not bad.

I put little circles of tape on the back of each of them, and then I open the trunk to that baby powder smell which is overpowered by a deeper smell of rot.

I hold my breath and clear my mind, fixing his dead eye by sticking the cut out against it and then twisting the cardboard a little bit so that the eye is lined up.

I've made a bigger circle of tape on the back of the second eye because it is going to have to get something at the edge to stick to. The hole, I see, is leaking some clear and bloody liquid I don't want to think about. I hold my breath and I press the cardboard eye down and the bloody liquid squishes out from the sides. I gag and adjust the eye and stand back.

I let out my held breath.

And then I really look at him.

The eyes are too small, and the color is not as good as I thought it was, but what is there is better than that black and red hole, and better than that eye that was his exactly but was clearly dead.

You want a man that can protect you from the world, that can stand between it and you.

There was an older man at the grocery store when Jack was gone on a trip. He followed me around looking at me out of the corner of his eye. I felt sorry for him and I appreciated his attention, and so I talked to him. His eyes were sad and you could see how they would grow appreciative. His place was large and it was clean from a maid that came twice a week. He was going to make dinner, but I told him to go to the bed. He was surprised because, like most men, he thought he had to trick a girl into fucking him.

All his muscles were slack. George might not be wonderfully built like Jack, but he was in better shape than this man. I told him to lean back and I pulled down his underwear and saw that he had gray hair there, even though the top of his head wasn't much gray. His cock head was all shiny with pre-come and I began to suck him. He kept trying to sit up but I'd push him down. I wanted to make him come so that I could go, but it seemed like he never would. Finally, I told him I needed him to come, and when I started sucking him again he put a hand on top of my head and starting thrusting his hips up. It took about half a minute. There wasn't much come and it was bitter. I told him I had to get home. His face was very sad and looked older than it had before, older even than I imagined my father's looking.

When Jack came back from his trip, I remember watching him sleep that first night and for many nights after and wondering why he didn't know what I had done.

I'm looking at these eyes I've made for him and thinking about how his real eyes are lost forever and thinking about the idea that if I hadn't known it before I'd fucked that other man, I knew afterwards that Jack could never shelter me from really much of anything.

I'm queasy. Maybe it's the smell, or the fatigue. Or maybe it's this strange sort of *déjà vu*: familiar things that don't really register until after I've passed them.

And then it's clear: I know this place.

I suppose I was probably trying to trick myself into thinking I didn't.

I am not that far, maybe an hour and a half, from where I grew up and where my parents still live. I haven't intended or not intended to come this way. It's just that here I am.

I know this stretch of interstate and I know these towns and I know where the turn off is if I want to stop and see my parents.

As far as I can imagine, there is no good reason for that.

I haven't been to my parents' since George and I came back that first Christmas after I left. That was the only real demand I think he ever made on me. He knew that I'd come home to live with my parents when I found out I was pregnant, and that after I gave birth to Danny Boy, I stayed there. I'd been two years in college. I learned a lot of things, amongst them how much boys like to fuck, and, at the same time, I learned that it was hard to find one that I wanted to stick with.

My father somehow knew that I was getting to know a lot of boys. Maybe all fathers know that. He said that I was probably trying to find him somehow, and that I wouldn't, and that it was natural for me to seek him that way, but that also it was danger-ous. Maybe he was right. That was seven or eight years ago; my father was a lot younger then. He still seemed to me the most perfect man in the world. My mother told me that I better watch out or I'd end up just another campus slut. When I had to come home and tell them I was pregnant.

Sometimes, my mother thought Danny was hers. Sometimes, she made me think it, too. Sometimes, I didn't feel as if I was old enough or that I knew enough to have him. Looking back, I know that thinking that way was the biggest mistake I've made. The right answers were probably in my own heart and head and probably always had been, but I didn't know that then. Now I face the fact that none of the bad things would have happened if I'd trusted myself.

What it all boils down to is that, looking back, I know it wasn't natural to have my mother involved.

Looking back, I guess we all paid the price for it, me and my mother coming together again after I'd been away.

That was when my father really started to age. And Danny Boy died.

Anyway, George thought he ought to start forging bonds with my family. "We've been serious a long time," he said. "Don't you think I should meet your mother and father?"

I'd been thinking that maybe we could pretend I never had a family, that there was nothing behind me, that everything started in Atlanta. But going to see my parents was the only thing I'd seen George adamant about, and so we went.

At first, they seemed distant, but by the end of the weekend he had my mother laughing. Before we left, my father took me aside and said that he loved me, and that he thought I'd made a decent catch, and that he hoped George knew what a perfect woman I was.

At the door for goodbyes, my mother whispered to me that she hoped I didn't mess it up. She said it loud enough for George to hear, and I saw his face get red. I was more embarrassed for him and the way he was blushing than I was for myself or my mother.

When I left George, I didn't call my parents. I figured something had really finally ended between me and them. My life was supposed to be about Jack then; that's what I told myself.

Sometimes, I tried to talk to Jack about Danny, but he didn't seem to be able to understand, as if Danny was just a character in a story and whoever I had been when all that happened was just a character, too, which, to be honest, is how I sometimes feel about it.

Then Danny's birthday came, and I guess it made me feel like I needed something from my parents after all, because as much as I could pretend nothing bad had ever happened, or that even nothing at all had happened, sometimes I couldn't avoid remembering and feeling. So I called. They didn't even know I had left Atlanta and wasn't with George, and so I told them that I'd moved to New Orleans and was happy and living alone.

"I knew you'd mess it up," my mother said.

"He was too old for her," my father said.

"She doesn't need a god. She doesn't need a piece of art. She just needs a man. The first one she gets who treats her like a woman instead of a slut, and what does she do? She messes it up."

"Well," my father said, but that was all. I could picture him, old faced on the extension in the study, and it shut me up, too.

He's got diabetes now. A few months ago, they had to cut off one of his feet. The other one is going to have to be cut of eventually, too. My mother told me that he hobbles around on a cane.

I know I am close to home, but I don't want to see him like this, and I don't want to see her at all.

I fill up and pay with the credit card at a gas station that wasn't here the last time I was. There are a lot of new things in this area, housing developments and businesses to serve them. The turn off is in another fifteen miles and I'm still telling myself I'm not going to take it.

The last time I spoke with my father, he said, "I know you don't want to come up here. I know why."

For a moment, I thought he meant that he knew that I didn't want to see him, but then I realized he meant I didn't want to go back home because of my mother. Though we have never talked about it, I know that he knows what she did.

And I know she couldn't help it, but that doesn't mean I can forgive her.

In her there is a rage. Probably she was born with it, or maybe somebody beat it into her.

It could be that I had on old socks or that I'd missed the bus or that I'd gotten into trouble at school or that I was snapping my gum. It could be that I "sassed" her, though I tried not to do anything that would seem sassy. Though I tried very hard to not miss busses or snap my gum.

The thing was, no matter what you tried not to do, there was always something. The thing was, my mother's rage could be about just about anything.

She never hit me in front of my father, but she hit me a lot. He pretended he didn't notice the darkness in the house after my mother had had an episode. He pretended he didn't notice the marks. I think he liked to get me out of the house so that I could be away from my mother. Sometimes, she seemed to feel bad afterwards. Once in a while she even told me that she'd probably gone too far.

When my father told me he knew I had good reasons for not coming back, he said, "I don't blame you. Don't let anybody tell you you owe anything to the dead or the dying, Baby Girl. And I know you're going to think I'm telling you this as a way of making you feel guilty, but I really mean it. You don't ever need to come to this place again. It probably wasn't good for you here for a long time and it probably won't ever be."

That was a week before they cut his foot off.

That's the exit, and I go right past.

This is a good thing.

I'm unburdened. My parents are behind me. My childhood, with the things I love and hate about it, is really gone.

This all means I'm ready to start absolutely fresh. No memories of consequence. No mementoes to lug around.

I couldn't be more sure of my new life with George.

Couldn't be more sure of what I've done to get onto this road to freedom.

Just couldn't be more sure in general.

And I feel this way for at least a mile.

Then I see a roadside advertisement for pickles, a little girl trying to take the top off the jar. She looks so determined that eventually she'll get it: she wants to so badly she has to.

I don't know why, but it makes me wonder if you really can put everything behind you just like that. In this pause, I remind myself that I'm in a car, not an airplane, and that maybe I chose this particular journey for a reason. I'm not supposed to go past. What I need to see, I don't know. Not Danny Boy's grave, which I haven't seen since the funeral. I don't need to see my father's canes, his absence of a foot. I don't need to see my mother's sour face.

I don't know what I need to see.

Just the same, I need to go back.

I turn through the grass medium and come up on the other side and start back, going east for the first time since I left.

Jack doesn't seem as stiff as he did before, and I think that maybe sunglasses would be the best bet concerning his eyes, which aren't right, or even close to it. How could they be?

This is in front of my parents' house, and here I am peeking in on Jack.

The sad thing is that in general, he looks better than he did the last time I saw him. This is sad because it means he's at the end of *rigor mortis* and now he's really going to start to decay.

Beneath the baby powder smell is his death smell, stronger.

I close the trunk quickly so it won't get on me and follow me in. There's enough death here already.

Why I'm checking on him, I'm not sure. Why I'm here, I still don't know.

There's the house. You could say it looms.

Inside it are my parents. I don't know what you could say about them.

Stumbling toward me with a cane in each hand is my father, grossly pale, his hair an ugly color of gray.

Patches of whitish stubble stand out from his face where he's shaved badly. There is a bruise on his cheek and one that is crusted up over his eye. He grins sort of sheepishly, and I wonder if he's gotten the bruises falling or if maybe my mother has started hitting him.

I don't look at where his foot should be; I don't want to see whatever it is he has there now. My mother stands there in a black dress with her arms folded, watching as my father and I embrace. She is shaking her head and I suppose it is with disgust.

"Baby Girl," my father says.

"Daddy."

"You're doing what now," my mother asks, "showing up out of the blue like this?"

"I've been driving," I say.

"You look a mess."

"It's been a long trip."

"The hurricane," my father says. "She's evacuated."

"Of course."

After a still moment, my mother comes forward and puts her hands on my shoulders and squeezes. She then leans forward as if she is going to kiss my cheek, though she does not kiss it. "What kind of trouble are you in?"

"I'm not in trouble."

"How long are you staying?"

"Just the night."

My father's face falls. My mother arches her eyebrow.

"What happened to the man?"

"Man?"

"Don't pretend you don't know what I'm talking about."

"George?"

"We all know what happened with George. You couldn't keep him."

"What man?"

"There's always a man. What happened to him?"

I imagine myself saying, "Actually, I killed him. Come on out and I'll open the truck so you can have a look. He's still handsome."

Instead, I say, "There is no man."

My mother and father stare at me. I feel a sense of expectation, the kind you know you can never meet. I know this, and I know that my father's falling apart and never was much of a savior anyway, and I know that my mother is a bitch and isn't getting any better, but despite knowing all of this, I want to fulfill their expectations anyway. I want to let them know about almost all of it, as if they could just understand my fairy tale, it would be a little better.

I guess we're always looking to find the pieces that are missing, to complete the picture.

I want to say: "Mother, you're right. There is a man. But he wasn't right. I'm going back to George. I'm driving to Seattle to be with him. Isn't it grand?"

But I know that in reality, even if she saw how positive it was, my mother would not be able to say so. In reality, my mother cannot feel happy for me.

It's just that I can't help wanting her to feel it.

There are all the things I want to say, as if they'd matter.

That we'll have a winter wedding.

That George and I will wake and sleep in joy, the way everybody has wanted to, always.

I just can't help it. I begin to make a picture in my head of both my parents at the wedding, smiling happily for me the way mothers and fathers smile for girls on television.

My father could give me away. The way fathers do.

Then I remember that my father's other foot will be gone by then. His face will probably be more bruised.

Everything will be worse.

The frown lines on my mother's face will be deeper, the darkness in her eyes blacker.

My parents are past the point of hope.

It's absurd to imagine the real them in Seattle. It's absurd to imagine them any place but here.

So I get my epiphany. So I get to understand why I couldn't just pass this place.

I had to stop and say goodbye, even if they don't hear me say it.

The lights are low because they hurt my father's eyes.

We're sitting in the living room and I'm squinting to see things. Then I stop because I don't really want to see any of it, not them or their things, not up close, not anymore, not at all.

"Light sensitivity," my mother says, shaking her head. "He's sensitive to so much. There's hardly a thing that doesn't bother him."

While my mother works on dinner, my father and I talk about the way life was, only we only talk about the good stuff, as if that is all there was. "Everything has changed here," he says. He goes toward the cabinet for the photo album, but along the way one of his canes gets caught up on something so that he stumbles a few steps and then falls completely. I don't know what to do. My mother comes rushing in and looks at him and then at me and rolls her eyes. She helps him up and he sits on the overstuffed chair, panting.

"I'm sorry," he says.

I know I should say he doesn't need to apologize, but I can't say it. I can't say anything. My mother comes back in with plates and puts one in front of my dad and one in front of me.

"He can't get around in the kitchen," she says.

He smiles another apology at me. She goes out and comes back with her own plate of food. The meat looks bloody and the peas look pale and the potatoes look lumpy. I have no hunger. My mother stirs her food around her plate and then lays her fork down.

So my father is the only one to eat. He does it slowly and with a focus and you can hear the knife and the fork on the plate, and his lips opening, and his teeth clinking together, and the slack muscle moving in his jaw.

When my mother picks up my full plate, she gives me a small smile of approval.

My father leans back and I see more color in his cheeks than before. I am happy for this and for the smile my mother has given me.

"I'm going to help Mom," I say. "Can I get you anything?"

"Nope." My father winks at me. He always used to do that. I love a man that winks, but I don't think many men do that anymore.

As I get up, I lean over just to touch him and I see on his forearm are bruises in the shapes of fingertips.

The rush of anger I feel is completely unexpected, as if all the anger I might have had at my mother has come back with full force, like an army of ghosts.

My mother loads the dishwasher and I watch.

"Why is dad bruised?"

She folds her arms and looks at me. "How do you think he'll get around when they cut off the other foot? I wish either of you had any idea of what it is like when everybody around you messes everything up."

"Why does he have all those bruises?"

"You have no idea what it's been like being your mother or his wife. You think you've been a good daughter? You think he's been a good husband? Do you think this is how it is supposed to be?"

I put my hands over my ears, but I can still hear her.

She says, "What is wrong with you?"

I take my hands away. "You're what's wrong with me."

Her mouth is open in an expression of surprise. Before she can speak, I say "You think you ever showed me love? You were jealous of me the day I was born, probably because of some look in Daddy's eye that he hadn't given you for years because of what you'd become."

So I get my real epiphany: I came here so that I could finally know what I've just said, and so that I could say it. I came here so that I could face the fact that my mother never loved me, and the fact that she never will.

"What I'd become?" she sputters.

"Who's the last person you brought joy to, and when was that?"

"You little bitch. You ungrateful, smug little bitch. I brought joy to Danny Boy and he was the only person that deserved it."

I scream. "I deserved it, too! I deserved it first!"

"You killed Danny Boy!"

"No, Mother, you killed him."

He was allergic to bee stings. We didn't know—who would guess something like that? Dad had hung up a bee catcher. They'd follow some scent up a little funnel that opened up into a plastic container they couldn't get out of. Then they'd die of hunger or thirst or loneliness or whatever. The first time I saw a live bee in there, I felt bad for it. I unhooked the trap from the tree and then took it out in the field behind the house. Then I unscrewed the funnel thing and let the bee out. He had an angry buzz by then, and he dove at me. I fended him off with my hands. Then he went buzzing away from me, back up toward the house. For some reason, I knew I ought to run after him. I heard a scream before I got there. On the porch was my mother leaning over Danny. He was lying there, kicking and spitting. A little ways away, I saw the bee back down on the splintery wood twisting about in the same way Danny was. I stepped on the bee and felt it crunch away to nothing. Danny didn't have on his pants, just his pajama shirt. Mom hadn't taken the phone away from her ear, though she was no longer talking to whoever she had been talking to.

I yelled at her. "He was supposed to be inside."

She threw the phone at me, but it missed and broke against the railing. A piece came up and cut me beneath my eye.

Danny continued to kick for a little while longer and then started to still. By the time the ambulance got there, he was dead.

My mother and I glare at each other. I can see in her face my own face, especially in the eyes, the way I look when I am angry, but age has made her ugly and I will never age like that, and I will never look as ugly in my anger as she does in hers.

And anyway, when I'm finished with this journey I will not have cause for anger any longer.

"The only good thing about that awful cunt of yours was that Danny Boy came out of it. You never wanted that boy anyway, and so you killed him," my mother hisses. "With your ineptitude, you've murdered your own son..."

I slap her. It has to be the most unexpected thing she's experienced, the same way that what I did to Jack had to be the most unexpected thing that had ever happened to him. My mother's eyes fill with tears, but they are of rage. She raises her hand, but I slap her again and her hand drops. She turns her head and starts screaming for my father.

"Don't," I say, but she keeps screaming. I can hear him coming on his canes and his fake foot. I'm not afraid of what he'll do to me. I just don't want to see him. He always wanted to believe each of us could love the others cleanly, that we could be the family he'd been taught to believe in; I know this is the final death of that hope. I slap my mother again, harder this time so that her head turns and she lets out a little cry.

It feels as good as anything I've done or imagined doing.

Then I go through the door and down to the car and have trouble getting the keys in the lock. My father comes out on the porch and starts yelling for me to come back. I can hear my mother screaming at him from inside. Then she comes into the doorway. I get the car door open and sit down.

"Please come back, Baby Girl," my father cries.

"Don't you ever come back!"

My father turns and lifts one of his canes and then staggers toward my mother with it. I start the car and push on the gas. My father starts to swing his cane toward my mother. She kicks my father's leg. It buckles. I am going forward now and I don't look back to see if my father has managed to hit her, and I don't look back to see him finish falling.

How stupid I feel, lost in my own neighborhood.

Not that it's my neighborhood anymore.

All I think I want is the interstate, but every time I go to make a turn, I have the feeling that it is the wrong way. Then I turn back the other way and feel as if I were right the first time. No matter which way I end up going, I know it's wrong.

I know what Jack would say: a reoccurring character dilemma.

That internal conflict you have to overcome before the character arc can be complete. In my case, it's self doubt.

New homes, tall and mostly white, with large windows softly lit. Everything seems perfect in this remake of the place where I used to live.

I try to think of what was here when I was a kid. I suppose it was a field or a forest. Maybe I rode my bike and played in this place. It's nothing like what I could remember. I can't imagine who has come here to live, though I'm certain that they are not the kind of people I've ever known.

The road hardly ever goes straight. It loops around and is crossed by other looping roads. At the far end of a cul-de-sac, at what looks to be the very edge of this neighborhood, I see what seems like the last home. It's three stories and made primarily of brick. On its porch are plantation style pillars. A sharp light shines above the doorway, and though no lights are on in the front windows, it is not fully dark inside. From the side of the house comes a patch of shaky light that must be made by a television picture. I wonder again at the nature of this place and the nature of the people in it.

I go a little bit back down the road that I came up, and then I park. I should not feel that people looking through windows will see me walking and recognize that I don't belong. I should not feel that people will assume that my motives are dark. Jack told me that a beautiful woman isn't really attractive unless she feels it, and that a plain woman who feels attractive acts appropriately and thus becomes it. In some way or another, he was trying to direct me with those comments, but I don't know what he was saying: that I was beautiful but didn't act it, or that I wasn't beautiful but did.

Anyway, I try now to feel as if I belong so that anybody who sees me will believe I do.

I walk up to the front porch just as if I'm going to climb the steps and knock on the door. As if these are my relatives or friends who have invited me to come to their new neighborhood and see how a new life starts.

Without checking for witnesses, I dash to the side of the porch. Then I turn the corner. Now I am in the darkness that is created between these two houses, and I feel a stronger sense of fear than I ought to. I have to remind myself that there is nothing really dangerous here, nothing truly bad that can happen to me. I make my way down the side wall, peeking through windows as I go. Through each of them, I see what I expect, a house in good order: furniture that seems perfectly shaped and placed and settled, with hanging pictures of people that if I could see them would prove to be smiling sincerely, books on shelves that if I could read them would prove to be just the right books.

Then there is the window with the light coming through it. Inside is a large screen television. Opposite of it is a couch. A man and a woman sit on it, watching the television. It must be something funny they are watching, because the woman laughs. The man looks at her and laughs, too. Then he looks back at the TV. They are not much older than I am, or they may even be the same age, roundish people who look calm. Somewhere above them, children must sleep. Two, I guess. A dog on the floor. A goldfish in a bowl.

Eventually, they lean closer to each other and her chin is pressed against his shoulder. He turns from the television and looks down at the top of her head. She doesn't even know that he's looking at her, but she's smiling anyway, a good and real smile.

I know what this is: this is what love looks like.

She lifts her face toward his and I imagine she smiles more broadly, though I can't see her mouth. He smiles, too. It's sort of goofy, but still, this would make a good picture.

They kiss, and her body shifts, looking a bit squishy. When she turns back to the television, I realize how heavy her face is around the cheeks, how sunken her eyes seem in all that flesh. His face is leaner, finer, and for a moment, I want to begrudge her him, but I know better.

They began kissing again, more deeply now. I see his hands are moving across her back and soon he's touching her breasts. She pushes into him so that he leans back and, as he does, his hands move up under her shirt. After a moment, he lifts it, so that her torso is bare except of her bra. She stands up and looks down at him. He sits there looking up at her.

I can see the thickness to her arms and the thickness of her belly, which hangs out over the waistline of her pants. He doesn't seem to mind. She undoes her bra and lets it slide down her arms and then she folds her arms across her breasts as if she is shy, but I guess she is only playing at shyness.

The man opens the buttons of his shirt and stands up to take it off. His skin is very white and flesh hangs over his hipbones in a way that makes him look deformed.

They are terribly far from perfect, but there is something beautiful about them anyway.

They embrace again, his arms around her and hers around him, and their faces coming together. These are slow kisses with hunger. After a little while, he begins to work her pants down until they catch at her knees. Her panties are pinkish and stretched wide across her ass. His hands knead the flesh there. After a little while, she hops around to get her pants the rest of the way off. He works his pants off, too, and then his underwear.

There is nothing graceful about any of what they've done, but it is still lovely to watch.

I realize that I would be her, even if it meant taking her figure and face and losing my own.

I can see his penis standing out at an angle, like something caught between rising or falling, a short cock and not very thick. She lies back on the couch looking at him as if he is the only man with the only penis in the world. Then he gets in between her legs and pushes inside of her. Her hands clasp together on his back. He begins moving against her, his ass puckering up and then flattening and then re-puckering with the movement.

Jack and I watched people have sex before and people watched us have sex. At those times, there always felt something obscene about it, though the obscenity of it excited me momentarily.

There is nothing obscene in this couple's lovemaking, though, and there is nothing obscene about me witnessing it.

I realize how wet I've grown and slip my finger into my panties and begin to play with my clit. I wonder if I'll be able to tell when they come and if I can come with them. I see her hands clutching and un-clutching and for the first time I can hear her. She is saying, "Yes," in a voice that is growing louder and louder, and she is saying, "More." It feels like my own voice. In fact, maybe I am saying these things too.

It's not very long until I'm close to coming.

Then I hear a strained voice behind me. "Fuck yes..."

When I turn toward the voice, I see that on the back porch of the house behind me is an older man, watching me watch the couple. He has his cock out and is stroking it. After a moment, his face goes awful, as if he's been shot and his shoulders hunch in. Come flies out of the tip of his cock. I pull my hand out of my panties and push myself against the wall. He shivers and then looks at me and raises his eyebrows.

"Nothing better than young love."

"Sick man," I say. "Sick, sick man."

He breathes heavily for a second and then leans toward me and leers. "You don't think they're putting on that show for me?"

"They wouldn't even have you for coffee," I say. "You are a disgusting man and I hope your house burns and that you burn with it."

In fact, I can see his house in flames. I can see him stumbling from it with fire eating his hair and skin. I can see it so well I can almost smell it, flame and char and smoke.

"What makes you any different than me?"

"What?"

"You and me, doing the same thing..."

My impulse is to leap at him. He looks at me, unable to imagine me hurting him. If he only knew what I'd done to Jack. If he only knew I'd just come from repeatedly slapping my mother. If he only knew that now I know how to come at the things that come at me and tear them down before they can hurt me anymore.

But right now, I'm not going to hurt the man. Nobody is going to burn his house.

I don't stop running until I am at my car. When I'm in, I turn around to see if the man has followed me, but he has not.

What he said was a lie. What that couple did, they did in innocence of someone like him. Even of someone like me. They were beautiful, and even the ugliness that sick old man on the porch brought could not ruin that beauty.

That's what I tell myself.

Right now, everything is clear to me.

Decomposition

I see the right roads. I find my way to the interstate.

This is the late night again, and I'm driving and it feels good to be driving.

Jack wanted to fuck me and a friend of mine, but the way he made it sound, he wanted to see the two of us fuck around with each other. Jack worked with words and he could make things seem the way he needed them to.

To talk me into fucking my friend, he told me that thought it would be exciting for him to watch women having sex in the flesh instead of on television. Furthermore, he said, it was less about feeding that excitement than it was about the idea that he wanted to open something up to me that I craved.

The way he made it sound, that he would get off watching, it would be a byproduct of him freeing me from some societal restraint I'd been wanting to push against.

She was our neighbor, and the two of us could sit for long periods of time without talking or needing to.

Jack started months before anything happened by whispering to me while we made love. He'd create fantasies involving other women and eventually he got to her. Dirty talk was his system for introducing all his kinks. He'd tell stories about doing things while we were fucking and he'd later say that my pussy got wetter than normal when he told the story. This, he'd say, was proof that whatever it was he was talking about was something I wanted as much as he did, if not more.

You find yourself being fucked in places you never thought you'd let somebody even see.

You find yourself putting your tongue in places you never thought you'd want to put your tongue.

You find yourself with a dildo in your ass and one in your mouth while he fucks you.

You find yourself doing all kinds of things.

For some of those things, I'm not going to say with certainty that he was wrong. I can see this complexly. I can see that he was not total darkness and badness and that he did not fully control me and that some of what happened between us was because of who I am and what I want.

The neighbor woman lived across from us. She has black hair and her lips were nearly black, too. Her ex-husband kept her kids and sent her money and that's what she lived off of. She came over often to drink tea with me in the afternoon. I never told Jack, but I got the sense from what she said she didn't really like him. He told me that he got the impression that she wanted to have sex with me. He told me that I wanted the same thing.

The idea was that he would watch and masturbate.

She kissed my mouth and licked my breasts and rolled her fingers around my clit. Then I went down and kissed the flesh between her pussy and thigh in just the place I get shivery when it's kissed on me. She swung her body around so that her pussy was still against my face but now her face was against my pussy, too. Her pussy lips were thick and very red and everything about her down there seemed swollen. I felt both repulsed and turned on, so that I pushed my head back into the mattress first and then just as quickly tilted it up, closing my eyes and working my tongue inside of her.

The way she sucked my cunt was better than the way anybody has. It was so good I stopped licking her and just focused on the sensation she was giving me. After awhile, we sat up and she began to kiss and finger me.

Jack watched and beat himself off, but I saw where his focus really was. He was watching her. He got closer, and I knew what he wanted. I brought her head over and she sucked his cock. He fingered her pussy.

I thought I'd been a step ahead, because I knew all along that though he kept telling me it was something he wanted to help me do for me, it was really for him, but the truth was, I was a step behind, because I hadn't realized in time that the whole experience was about him getting something fresh. She sucked him until he came.

When she went back to her apartment he held me, but he was silent and still and unsatisfied.

After that, I didn't ask her over for tea or answer when she called. She moved eventually. That was my only real friend in New Orleans.

Dec   osition

As I drive, I tell myself that I will be like the woman in the house back there. What I see between her and her husband was my future with George, the window my crystal ball. Ahead of me, there is a man who will look at me with adoration.

That man will be George.

And I will look at him the same way.

Our lovemaking will have no edges, nor will we feel the need for them.

We will always make love. We will not even need to fuck.

I'm glad for the interstate.

I'm glad for the stars and the moon.

I'm glad I've got a full tank of gas and that if I'm tired I'm not even aware of it. I'm glad that all this is real, that Jack is dead and that roads and highways and interstates really do lead places they are supposed to. I know we are taught to be thankful for our blessings, but I don't think I need to thank anybody. It's enough just to be glad.

It's enough to be going west or north or both.

It's enough to have my troubles mostly behind me.

I don't need to thank anybody, but I say it anyway, *Thank you*, and I look at my own two eyes in the rearview mirror. A heat pulses through my stomach, the way I feel when I look at somebody I think I love.

So I love myself, that's what I've learned, that's the final epiphany I get from stopping home one last time.

DAY III.

This interstate cuts right through the mountains, turning red in the rising sun.

I think of Johnny Appleseed and Snow White, happy trails through kind forests.

Then I imagine Smaug, the dragon in the picture book I used to read as a kid, yellow-chested and red-winged. He rises hungry and mad, and you know there is no way past him.

I go between seeing good and seeing bad.

Beauty and ugliness.

I'm certain, then I'm not certain. Positive then negative.

The sun is rising, but I'm moving out of its light and into the mountain shadows.

Jack was always agonizing over the right word. As I drive further into the mountains, I get mine: daunted. I know where I am in my journey. I'm in my period of doubt. What I tell myself is that it will make me stronger. If I ever tell my story, and who knows, maybe someday I will, this is a necessary part.

The interstate seems to me too narrow, and I can't help the impression that I'm in the valley of death. Up at the top, everything sparkles, everything is fine, but down here I am in the darkness.

Into this place, the dragon will swoop.

This is all just my mind playing tricks on me, but realizing that doesn't mean I can escape its impressions.

What I need is higher ground.

A dirt road out of a little town in which I buy fuel cuts upward. It may seem I'm losing track of my journey, but I tell myself this, too, is part of it.

The road crosses over other dirt roads, some of them overgrown.

Eventually, I reach a lake, small and flat, light blue. The road goes around it, and though I know I'll end up right back where I started, I take the road. There are pull-offs along the shore with stone rings for fires and weathered picnic tables. On the far side there are two cabins that seem empty. When I've finished the circle, I get out of the car and go down the little trail to the shore of the lake. The cabins are across from me now. A trail leads down from one of them to a little dock. No boat is visible, but there must be one in the shed between the cabins.

I think I know why I am here.

I kneel down and wash my hands in the lake and then splash the water onto my face. Jack would present this as a baptismal moment, but for me, the cold of the water simply feels good.

I look out across the water at the cabin and the shed and the dock. The shed is probably locked, but I've already proven that I can get past barred doors. I used to be the kind of person that thought that everything happens for a reason. Then Danny Boy died and I quit thinking that way.

But maybe it's true after all.

Maybe everything happens for a reason. There is a reason I found and followed the road. And there is a reason this lake exists, and a reason that the cabin has been built and a boat put into its shed.

It would be impossible for there to be no boat in the shed.

I am here because I am supposed to be.

All this exists so that I can take Jack out and sink him.

I don't know if it's perfect timing—if I found the lake when I did because I was finally ready, or if it is that finding the lake has made me ready. It doesn't matter. Here is the lake. And here am I, ready.

It's been a long time I haven't seen him, since last night, when I arrived at my parents', eleven hours ago, I guess, but longer than that in some ways. Back up the trail, I rub my eyes, yawn, stretch, and open the trunk.

It's been over fifty hours since I killed Jack. He looks overly relaxed, slack in the cheeks and the jaw. One of the cardboard cut out eyes has shifted and I adjust it, but it doesn't help his appearance much.

I lean toward him, feeling soft, ready to whisper that it really is time for goodbye, ready to accept the pain necessary for real release.

A high-pitched noise comes from Jack, and then, from beneath the cardboard eye that covers the hole where Jack's eye would have been if Little Dear hadn't pecked it out, a fly emerges.

I know what it was doing in there. That fly was laying eggs.

I know those eggs will hatch.

I know that Jack will become a home for maggots.

I look again at the lake.

It is most certainly the time.

But instead of wresting Jack out of the trunk, I move away from the car. Then I'm kneeling, and my stomach feels like it's pumping, and my throat is open, and no matter how much I don't want to vomit, I know I'm going to. I check to make sure I'm out of view of the trunk. I don't want to throw up where Jack could see or hear or smell it, even though he can't see or hear or smell. Even though he is the one who is disgusting. This is how well he trained me. He hated things of the body. When I was sick he'd leave the apartment, once for two days. Each of us had our own bathroom, and if I'd even pee in mine with the door just a crack open, he'd yell.

Jack would occasionally fuck me in the ass. He'd do this in the dark. After coming, he'd go immediately for a shower, which he'd take in darkness as well.

You think I don't know what that was all about, Jack? What do you expect to happen when you stick your cock in somebody's ass? Of course they're going to get shit on you.

If you can't handle that kind of intimacy, then you should have been satisfied with normal sex.

I'm kneeling by the lake, retching with fatigue, retching over the thought of maggots and shit and my decaying ex.

Then I just fold my hands over my belly. I'm not going to throw up after all. Maybe this is my will kicking in, or maybe it's just luck. Maybe it is just that as my mouth fills with the taste of whatever is coming, I can't stand the thought of the half-digested stuff in my stomach splattering on these smooth stones, this blue water.

I stand up.

The lake looks so calm and pretty, and Jack is so dirty and sick, I'm not sure that in good conscience I can bring them together.

I go back up the trail and close the trunk of the car and then walk over to the picnic table and sit. I lean forward and put my head down on my forearms. This time I'm aware of sleep coming down. Then I'm not aware of anything.

When I try to wake, it is to the sound of a vehicle. I am vaguely aware of doors opening and closing and voices, but I cannot come back into the world. I want to ignore the sounds. I want just the pure black, and then it comes again. I don't know how long I'm in it, but eventually I recognize the feeling of something wrong and I know I must wake.

I can't.

As much as I didn't want to be awake moments ago, I can't bear the thought of not being awake now. If I can just move any part of my body, if I can wiggle my toe or twitch a finger, I'll make it. I get more and more desperate but cannot connect myself to my body. Then it feels as if my eyes have burst, they are so full of light. Each of my muscles is taut. I'm sitting up.

Standing on the other side of the picnic table and staring at me is a small girl in jeans and a sweatshirt. She's got pigtails. This is what I looked like as a child. Perhaps I am still dreaming. Perhaps I have conjured her, some old me, and she has some wisdom or well wishes for my journey. I could use them right now.

"Hi," she says.

"Hello."

"Something smells over here."

"How old are you?"

"I'm seven."

Somebody calls, "Michelle? Michelle!"

She turns her head toward the voice.

"That's my mother." The girl raises her hand. Then I see the woman coming through the trees. "Michelle, you can't just wander off like that."

The mother comes up to the girl and shakes her head, and then the mother looks at me and gives a small smile and says, "Sorry."

"It's okay. I was just taking a nap."

I see her nostrils widen slightly and I see her eyes study me. She continues to smile, but now something uncertain has moved into her eyes. She sniffs more openly. After a moment, she puts her hands on the girl's shoulders and moves the girl away from the table.

"Did you find her?" There is a man coming through the trees. He is tall and wears a flannel shirt. I'd call him handsome. About thirty yards behind him is an SUV and large tent with white walls that look to be made of canvas. His smile drops when he sees the face of his wife and it drops further when he looks at me. He shifts his chin down in kind of nod.

"Go on back to the campsite," he says.

"Daddy..."

"Go right now."

The mother takes the girl by the arm and starts to lead her away.

"Bye," the girl says.

"Goodbye."

The man watches them until they are out of his hearing. Then he says to me, "Are you all right?"

"I'm fine."

"Are you sure nothing has happened to you?"

"I just fell asleep."

"Do you know where you are?"

"Of course I know where I am."

"You look like something has happened."

"All kinds of things have happened."

"Do you need to call somebody?"

"No."

He nods by bringing down his chin again, and I see something dismissive in it, the kind of motion Jack would make when he wasn't really listening because he already had everything figured out. I can see right through this man's flannel shirt. It's brand new. So is that tent. I bet everything he's brought is fresh off the shelves of some department store and that he doesn't know what he's doing here. He couldn't make it in these woods much better than I could. He's not the great man that he wants his family to think he is. He might be fooling himself, but he's not fooling me, just like Jack couldn't fool me forever.

"Listen, are you hungry?"

I've eaten very little since killing Jack, but I'm used to going off of little food. You've got to know how to keep your figure. I know how to draw my belly in. How to cinch my waist. How to make my arms and thighs thin and my collarbones stand out. I know this is what the world wants from me. I've done it most of my life. Sometimes, I ask myself: Why hasn't it been enough?

"Let me bring you a sandwich."

"No, really."

He looks doubtfully at me, and he looks at my car. I can't remember if I left the trunk open or not. If I did and he sees

Jack, I'll have to kill him. And his wife. And child. I suppose that is one of the prime questions of the story of this trip. How far would I go to properly make it?

No. Not me. I could never do that.

I don't think I could. I couldn't kill that little girl.

Anyway, his eyes move back to me and I look and see the trunk is closed.

"Please, I'll be right back."

I watch him walk through the trees and I get up and go to the car, feeling almost refreshed for my sleep. After I start my car, the man comes jogging up. I can just pull away, but I don't. I unroll the window. The man hands me a sandwich in a baggie.

"It's ham," he says.

"I don't eat ham."

"It's mock ham, actually. Vegetarian ham. Soy ham."

I nod. I see that in the baggie is not only the sandwich, but some type of bill folded up. I'm not angry at the man anymore. He's like my father, doing the best he could for me, handing me a gift. I understand he means to do good. I understand he means for his wife and child to see something good done. I understand that all together they mean to help.

"Thank you."

He nods, that same dip of the chin.

I begin to drive. The girl and her mother are in front of the tent. Each of them waves. I wave back.

The sandwich tastes enough like pig to call to my mind the pictures and movies of the decomposing piglet.

I'm on the interstate again and I throw the sandwich out the window, as hard as I can, so that it lands off the road, where an animal can eat it safely.

I unfold the bill, a fifty, and smooth it out on the seat beside me. The interstate winds along a river for a while and then begins to climb away from it, the grade getting steeper, my car beginning to struggle, other vehicles passing me.

What I'm feeling, I'm not sure. Certainly it is okay to feel nothing. To just drive. It's better than before, when I'd wavered between good and bad and then settled into that feeling of doom.

Soon, we're almost out of the trees, past the place they call timberline, close to the top of this mountain. The air coming in the windows feels fresh, the way you hear about mountain air feeling, and it's got autumn in it, my favorite time of year.

The way this is supposed to be about fresh starts, I know spring would be a better seasonal symbol, but this is not one of Jack's stories where everything works out in a way that makes the right meaning.

Aspen leaves are in colors of yellow and orange and brown. Some of them release and fall just as I'm passing, and I understand I've witnessed a one-time-only moment in the life of each of them. My car chugs. We're climbing, going up and up and up, slowly but steadily, so that it feels like we might reach the sky.

Beneath that fresh and autumn air smell is the smell of Jack rotting.

My head is light, I suppose from the smell and from the elevation. From lack of sleep and all this driving.

The Mustang, it feels kind of heavy, like Jack is an anchor in the trunk. I should have gotten rid of Jack, but I didn't.

Off to the left a little ways ahead is a large brown building. The mountainside above it has huge patches where there are no trees but only grass. It takes me a moment to realize that these are ski runs and that the building is a ski lodge. I see now a chair lift moving and a couple of people sitting in the hanging chairs.

There are a few vehicles in the lot.

The air is fresh, but thin, and I'm dizzy.

I'm going to pull over, just for a second.

The lodge has the feeling of a place abandoned, but there is a man reading a book in a booth.

He sells me a ticket without looking up for more than a moment. There is an open cut, the blood not really coagulated, coming from his nose, as if something started scratching inside of his nostril and worked its way out.

If I didn't quiet my mind, I would be telling myself that this is some ghost world, a place where Jack is more at home than I am.

I go to the base of the chairlift, where another man waits, also reading a book. I search his face for cuts but there are none. He seems to search mine as well. For what, I'm not sure.

Since he doesn't speak to me, I don't speak to him.

I've never done this before, in winter or in summer. My father talked sometimes about a ski vacation, but we never went. He took my mother once a year on a cruise and I'd stay with neighbors. It's odd—and maybe I'm just remembering it wrong—but I think I missed them when they were gone, even my mother.

The man gets up slowly and stands stiffly in a certain spot and then moves away and sweeps his hands toward that spot. After a moment, I realize that he has shown me what to do. I stand there, nervous about how this is supposed to work and not comfortable with the idea that nobody has said a single word to me.

"Is it scary?" I ask.

His face breaks into a smile and he shakes his head. Then he winks. I'm relieved by all these gestures, but when I see the chair coming, my impulse is to get out of the way. I have to will myself to freeze. The man steadies the chair and then holds it still, and when I don't react to it or him, he pulls me to sitting. The chair jerks and I start up.

"Goodbye," I say.

"Goodbye," he says.

It is odd to feel my feet pull away from the ground.

In no time at all, I'm too high to disembark. This, naturally, makes me want to get off the chair very badly. A couple passes on the other side, coming down, both in sweat shirts and big, mirrored glasses. They smile at me. I don't smile back. The grass is so green and pretty looking it is hard to imagine that you'd actually get hurt jumping onto it, but I know you would. I know that if something made me leap, I'd feel my bones break. Maybe I'd feel my soul start to lift.

This is, of course, no way to think. I'm on a chairlift, that's all. This is something people do all the time.

They do it for pleasure.

I'm having fun.

I'm relaxing.

I look behind me and the chair rocks a little. The building is far away. I can't even see the Mustang. It might as well not exist; in fact, nothing really does, just me, hovering in the air, on this stupid chair hanging stupidly from these cables, this place no person was meant to be.

I recognize this as the worst idea I've had on this journey.

I face forward again and the shifting of my torso causes the chair to rock more. When it goes as still as it feels like it will get, I tell myself that if this is the worst idea, then also it will turn out to be the most telling test.

That this is the crux moment.

I hum and ride and try not to think about how helpless I am. I hum and stare forward and try not to think of anything. I hum and hum and hum.

Then, in front of me, there's a little wooden booth with a porch on it and a hill sloping away from the porch to the beginning of the ski run. This is the real top of the mountain, all dirt and rock. I remember how the mountain tops looked in the sunlight this morning, like some magic place, but that's not how this real mountain top looks up close. It looks like the end of the world.

It looks like the place all the dead pass through before getting to the other side.

That I should make it back from here seems impossible.

The chair and the porch at the top of the little hill converge, so that it is possible for me to step off. In fact, that is exactly what I'm supposed to do. Other people have gotten off and they are just fine. I can see them, three of four walking safely on the trail below. A man is standing in front of the little wooden booth. Perhaps he is twenty-one or two, with his shaggy blond hair and blue eyes. I try to make him see that I'm stuck and that I need some kind of help, but he only watches me pass. He doesn't want to be a hero. Men don't really want that, but sometimes they play that role out so that they can get saved from something themselves.

George and I met two weeks after Danny Boy's funeral. I'd gone to the city and was crying in the streets because I didn't want to cry in front of my mother. Somebody came and sat down beside me. When I looked, it was a stranger, George, in town on business. He never tried to solve anything for me but only listened and then held me lightly. Within two months, I was living with him in Atlanta. That's its own little love story, until you get to the part about me going off with Jack.

And that doesn't have to be so awful. That can just be the obstacle that gives the story weight.

Like me on the chairlift, whipping around that big toothy wheel and leaving the place that is closest I got to safety.

I just think of George, the way I saw that he felt my pain when I expressed it. The way he didn't try to talk me out of it or fuck it out of me or do anything at all but listen and care.

George is getting me down the mountain, the way he got me off that bridge railing.

I'm hanging here from a chair and there is nothing natural in it, but I'm doing just fine, thinking about George. I was too young to appreciate him once, but now I'm not.

You're all right, I keep telling myself.

George loves you, I keep saying.

You're going to make it, I sing out.

Then I look down and get instantly dizzy. Colored patterns fill my head. I'm looking down, but I don't see anything. I forget where I am, what I'm doing, why I'm doing it. I forget even who I am. When I start to see again, most of these things come back to me. Where I am and why and who.

I see that I'm leaning too far forward, my body imbalanced, my brain becoming aware of it.

I could fall. I say this to myself three times, as if it's a chant that will keep me in place.

As the chair descends, I do not move.

The chair jerks as it starts to go around the big wheel at the base, and my feet drag on the ground. I try to stand up and then chair bumps me and I mean to take a step but it bumps me again.

"Hey," the man with the book says.

This time, I try to run. The chair keeps going. I stumble and roll over.

The man starts toward me and I get up, putting a hand in front of me. I hear myself laugh, and I take a couple of backward steps and stumble and fall again.

The book man keeps coming and I hear that I'm still laughing. I am on the ground. I am fine.

On the trail back to the parking lot, I have the sudden sense that Jack is gone.

I look around as if for him, or as if it is for someone who has taken him, or even just someone who has witnessed him going.

The couple from the chairlift sits on the open tailgate of their truck eating a picnic opposite of my car, their sunglasses in their hair. The woman is fat and eats with the kind of piggy hunger I'd never show a man. Her husband holds a big slice of watermelon, his belly hanging out of its dirty white t-shirt.

They pretend not to notice me, offended, I suppose, because I didn't wave back at them on the chairlift.

I'm offended myself, disgusted to the point of anger. There are all these things to be mad about.

I'm mad because I want to open the trunk but can't, at least not safely with the couple sitting there across from it.

I'm mad at Jack for having the kind of hold on me that makes me need to open the trunk to begin with.

I'm mad at George for not being strong enough in my mind so that I don't have to think about Jack.

I glare at the couple, mad at them not just because they make me feel like I can't open the trunk, but because of the way they eat, as if their only purposes in this world relate to digestion.

Maybe if I stand just so, I'll block their view of the body in the trunk when I open it. If there is a body.

Are you in there, Jack?

You can hear the rattling of the paper and the smacking of their lips.

I open the trunk slowly, really ready for it to be empty, as if the bulk of this trip is a dream I've had. As if I never killed Jack. As if I've left him alive down in New Orleans and he'll go about his merry life without me, an unbearable thought.

He's there, and all the weirdness of this place and this trip melts away and I'm just looking at a real corpse in the trunk of my car. Half a dozen flies stir but then resettle on him. His skin is more flaccid yet, and both cardboard cut out eyes are askew.

And he's smiling. He wasn't smiling before.

I know why he's doing it.

This is what you wanted, isn't it, Jack?

You want to guarantee George can't displace you. You want to demonstrate your hold on me. Just like I don't want you walking around smiling in New Orleans, you don't want me to have my happily ever after without you.

I hate you, Jack.

The tire iron is showing from behind him and I pry it out. I'm ready to strike his face with it hard, but then I can't. Call that weakness. I poke him in the side, hard. Call that a show of strength.

Against the blow, the flies scatter and buzz and a deeper smell comes off of him. I press the tip of the tire iron against the corner of Jack's lip and then I jerk down on it, causing the smile to crumple.

Then I close the trunk.

The man is watching me and the woman is rolling the garbage of their meal into a giant ball. The man sucks one and then another of his fingers and looks at them.

These repulsive people.

The tire iron hangs heavy in my hand. I can imagine how it would feel to strike the finger sucking husband and then his piggish wife. It would sink down through the fat and thud against their bones. I can imagine the way they would cry out, and I try to imagine whether or not that and the feel of striking them would satisfy me.

I get in the car and put the tire iron beneath the seat.

Call that restraint.

I can't think of the last time I've been in a tunnel, but I remember as a kid when I'd pass through them with my father, he'd honk the horn, even though my mother would tell him it was stupid and unsafe.

The tunnel I'm in is very long and goes right through the tip of the mountain. I press my hand against the horn, but it doesn't sound right, not that high-pitched giddy cry of our family car, but a low and heavy sound. There's that horn that is supposed to blare before the world ends, and I suppose that's what I'm hearing. But then the light that is the end of the tunnel grows larger, and I pass from the semi-dark into the fully bloomed day. I realize I'm still blowing the horn and it doesn't sound frightening anymore.

The interstate descends, a series of zigzags, and I coast them all the way down, until the roadway flattens out. I'm driving now through valleys that are tight enough to make me feel protected but not so tight as to make me feel claustrophobic.

Behind me is the mountain, the tunnel, all of that, and when I look in the rearview mirror, I know what a long way I've come.

If Jack didn't stink so much, I might have forgotten he is still with me.

The shop is made mostly of light green fiberglass.

This is in a mountain valley town, one of those perfect places where perfect people live.

Inside the flower shop there are rows and rows of trees and plants. An entire wall is lined with glass-doored refrigerators full of flowers. There are machines spitting out mist, giving the place that hokey look of jungles in old movies. On a wooden platform in a darkened corner are a dozen or so large tanks. I look at the fish, and whether they dart or drift, it seems to me that in their glass cages what you can really see in them is desperation, but there is nothing I can do to help them, so I simply turn away.

An Asian man and woman are behind the counter, looking so much alike that they could be brother and sister, but I guess them for husband and wife. They smile and nod almost in unison.

"Very pretty," the woman says.

"Thank you," I say.

Then I realize she is talking about the fish. I swallow my embarrassment and make my way between a row of little trees and up to the counter. "They are pretty, aren't they?" I say.

The woman smiles and the man rises. "May I help you?"

"I need the best smelling roses you have."

"A dozen roses?"

"Two dozen. No. Three."

"What color of rose?"

"Red. Half red. The other half white." I think this will be pretty. I think that if Jack had ever sent me roses, those would be the colors I would have most liked.

"How would you like them wrapped?"

"I don't want them wrapped. Just in a box. No baby's breath or anything like that. The box doesn't even have to be fancy."

The woman nods and makes her way out from behind the counter.

There is a little and old looking radio on the counter, either turned off or at least all the way down. I say to the man, "Do you know what happened in New Orleans?"

The man's eyes fall from mine. "Very bad," he says. "Very, very bad. Everything under water."

So the evidence of Jack's death has been washed away. The only proof is the body itself.

The woman comes back carrying three white boxes, each tied with a red ribbon. She sets them one by one on the counter.

The man asks, "Are you from New Orleans?"

If I weren't paying with the credit card, if I didn't think that somehow the man would be able to know I was lying, I would not tell him the truth. I nod.

"We only charge you for two of the dozen," the man says. "God bless you."

"Thank you," I say. "I'm going to Seattle. No disasters there. No floods. No hurricanes. No tornadoes. Not even fire."

"Oh, no," the man says. "Seattle is for the earthquake, the worst possible of all earthquakes."

"Seattle in trouble," the woman agrees.

It's a lie, an awful lie, the kind of lie some evil apparition offers the heroine along the road to the future she deserves.

I feel like shattering the glass doors on the refrigerators and snapping the heads off flowers and breaking the stems of plants and the trunks of the small trees. The man and his wife, smiling their stupid little smiles, this is their little false Eden, and what I'd like to do most is destroy it.

You can hear the bubbling of the tanks and the mist coming out of the machines. As I press my fingers into my eyes, I tell myself to be calm. I tell myself this couple wants me to feel bad about where I am going because they feel bad about where they are. They are trapped here in this strange light amongst this constant mist with the sounds of the bubbles in the fish tanks; they are stuck here pruning and watering and scooping out the dead, and they don't want to imagine someone going someplace better to be truly happy.

I pay without saying anything more and I take the flowers out to my car.

There are more flies than there were before. His eyes are hopelessly askew and hopelessly wrong in terms of color and size and shape.

I know what is going to happen soon. Bacteria will eat enough of his organ tissue away for the fluids inside to release into his body cavities. Then various gasses will cook up there. Sulphide and methane, bubbling up all kinds of force. Cells and blood vessels will cave in against the pressure, releasing more fluid, causing his torso and trunk to swell.

Fluid from his lungs will ooze out of his mouth and nostrils.

I can only do what I can do. I can only try to fix the eyes. Only try to deal with the smell.

Inside a convenience store is a display of cheap sunglasses, and I buy a pair, straightforward, with black frames and black lenses.

I've parked off to the side of the store, and I open its trunk and put the sunglasses on Jack's face. I close my eyes and try to clear my head. Then I open my eyes quickly to see what I would think of Jack if I'd just spotted him with no expectation of what I'd see. Jack looks better, good, even, and, in the shades, he looks sort of cool like he always wanted to think he was.

I open the boxes of roses and arrange them one by one around his head, all along his torso, the stems sticking between his body and the bathrobe, the blooms resting on his grayish flesh. Then I push several flowers—white and red and white and red—into the waistband of his pajama bottoms. When I stand back it looks to me as if the roses are growing out of him, and I like that, as if I've helped to recreate him, better than he was before.

I close the trunk. I have about ten roses left. These I put in the back seat to act as a filter between me and Jack.

As I'm getting back in the front seat, I hear my name. It's a female voice and I turn to it to see who's spoken.

There she is, Kimberly Barnes. For a moment, that's all that I think: her name, over and over.

In truth, I'm not even surprised. A light comes on like that for no reason in the dark and you know she isn't going to be completely out of the story.

"Oh my God," she says, "What are you doing here?"

Kimberly Barnes and I are sitting in an old fashioned style café drinking coffee, something I don't typically do because it stains your teeth.

Though I consider other methods, mostly, I'm thinking about the thermometer.

I'm thinking: the thermometer is not just old fashioned looking but actually old.

I'm thinking that out there on the porch is hanging a little vial of real mercury.

I'm thinking about the twin girls, Sara and Melissa, my neighbors, who when we are all about seven somehow got into some mercury one morning and were dead by nightfall.

I couldn't guarantee it, but I'm pretty sure Kimberly Barnes knows Jack is dead and knows that I've done it.

I'm thinking: I've got to get that mercury out of the thermometer and into her coffee.

There is new life waiting for me, and Kimberly Barnes, sitting across the table, is just another obstacle. She is thin, about twenty-five, with a plain face, the kind boys sometimes grow fond of. She keeps talking about Jack. She keeps asking questions.

Where is he? Why am I here? Isn't this a strange coincidence?

What you have to wonder is how much you should trust your first impulse.

What I have to ask myself is whether or not it means anything that her light came on just as I was pulling out, whether or not it means something more that twenty minutes ago she appeared from out of nowhere to stand behind me.

Coincidences are for books, the kind Jack wrote. This is real life and Kimberly Barnes and me being here, a couple thousand miles from where we were somehow both up at an odd hour, it's too much to seem reasonable.

She's telling me that she feels shattered by what has happened in New Orleans. She's asking me if I'm sure Jack is all right. Have I actually heard from him? She asks me again if he's really gone to Atlanta, as I claimed. She peers into my eyes as if she is trying to recognize a lie.

What is really going on in her mind, I may never know.

As for me: mercury. That's what I'm thinking.

Somehow, Kimberly Barnes gets to telling me her story. According to what she says, she grew up in this little mountain town. In this story, she always wanted to get out of here, the way everybody wants to get out of whatever place they are from. She'd gone to a state school for her undergraduate degree, but she was going home some weekends, all the holiday, for summer vacation. She had to get away for real.

I ask her about the flower shop, does Kimberly Barnes know of it? And Kimberly Barnes, she looks to be thinking on it, and then she nods and says that of course she does.

She continues to tell me about her story, about how happy she was to go far away for graduate school. About how over the course of this last year, she'd fallen in love with New Orleans. She'd found her place, and now it was drowned.

You've got to ask yourself about motivation. If she's not just spilling her guts, why does she tell me these things? If she knows about Jack, what is she up to?

She could be buying time. She could be trying to trick me into saying something.

She holds the coffee cup in both hands and looks perplexed as she brings it to her lips.

"Excuse me," I say.

"What?"

"I'll be right back."

"Okay." Her left eye seems to half close and shudder and then re-open. A movement like that, just about any movement, you can read it pretty much any way you like. Whatever you're thinking, you can make it fit.

Kimberly Barnes is truly having the tough time she's described. Or Kimberly Barnes is nervous because she thinks or knows that she is sitting with a killer.

Now she smiles, thinly, strangely. Maybe she's faking it. Or maybe this is just the way she always smiles, with a little crook at the corner and no warmth in her eyes.

I go out and walk down the porch and grab the thermometer, which comes away easily, leaving a burnt looking nail head. Then I walk down the steps off the porch. I take the tire iron out of the front seat and then open up the trunk. Flies rise and swarm and settle.

I hold the thermometer against the floor of the trunk and try to ignore Jack as I beat the tire iron against the thermometer. It cracks with the second hit, but not deeply enough for anything to come out.

Jack is looking at me, through those fake eyes and sunglasses, seeing me, seeing into me, seeing my intentions, knowing somehow that I'm going to kill Kimberly Barnes, one of his students, a girl who moved suspiciously close to us rather suddenly and has now, even more suspiciously, appeared here.

"She's in there, Jack," I tell him. "She thinks she's going to solve it."

I lift up the tire iron and hit the thermometer especially hard. The glass opens up. Mercury rolls out in a half dozen little red balls. It occurs to me that I have nothing to carry it in. I look around for a discarded plastic cup or something like that, but those kinds of things don't lie around in a town like this for long.

Then I hear my name called from the porch. Kimberly Bares is standing there looking at me.

"Is everything okay?"

"Yes," I say. "Yes." And then I simply scoop it up, all the mercury, and it melds in my palm into a jellyish ball.

It's all right, I tell myself. I'll wash my hands. It won't seep into me, not that quickly. I, the poisoner, am not myself going to be poisoned.

Everything is going just fine.

That's what I tell myself.

She's got another cup of coffee and my hand with that mercury is cupped under the table. We've been sitting for what feels like an awfully long time. When I let my brain acknowledge the mercury at all, I can feel it burning into me. This is just my imagination. Or I think it is.

Nobody here understands, according to Kimberly Barnes. All they see is that she is safe. Lucky girl, but she doesn't feel lucky.

I nod. My hand burns.

"I'm sorry, I'm just going on and on," she says. "It's the writer in me. You must know. Ja...Professor Wilson must be that way. Only what he says must be, I don't know, deeper. I don't want to sound like one of those gushy students, one of those fan club types, a little disciple. I just really respect him."

Maybe she thinks she found a friend in me, and this conversation and the coincidence from which it sprung is innocuous.

Maybe she's keeping me here waiting for the small town police to come by and collect me, and so I'm in danger.

Maybe she wants to see if I'll slip up and prove a theory she is almost sure of.

"When I think of our classroom, when I think of the way we'll never sit there again, that it all might be over, that I might never see him again...I don't know." She puts a finger to her eyes, not quite theatrically, but still, there is an air of falseness to it.

She rises, saying, "Excuse me."

As soon as she is out of sight, I drop the mercury into her coffee. It's like I'm releasing something hot. My hand still burns. As I began to rise to join Kimberly Barnes in the bath-room, where I can use soap and water on my hand, there is a sound from her purse that stops me. It is a cell phone ringing. I take it out, and it's recognizable.

My home number, I think, as if Jack is calling.

But no, just a New Orleans area code. I wonder how anybody can be calling from there, and who.

As I put the phone back in the purse, I see her open wallet. I take it out so that I can look at the driver's license.

On it is a local address.

I'm sure of this as long as I'm looking at it. Then I hear the bathroom door opening and I drop the wallet back in the purse and sit down. I tell Kimberly Barnes that her cell phone rang and then I say "Excuse me" and go into the bathroom and scrub my hand over and over.

Mercury poising: dizziness, nausea, fever. Some black door opens up and you want to go through it.

She's not touched her coffee. I could still put a stop to it.

The address was local. I think that's what I saw. If this is true, she might not have been lying. We might be sitting here out of coincidence after all. And she might be innocent of that knowledge of which I suspect.

She says, "I'm really, I don't know...I feel lucky to have bumped into you here."

She could just be a girl reaching out. Or she could be a girl playing tricks.

The question anymore is not about me trusting her, but about me trusting me. Really, if you look at the story of my life, maybe any life, that's what it comes down to.

Now mountains and their valleys are behind us. Here the ground is reddish and the foliage sparse. I drive throughout the afternoon in a sort of haze. Jack is back there in the trunk with his rotting roses. George is somewhere up ahead.

I am making time.

My hand, it sort of hurts, but this might just be in my mind.

I'm dizzy, the way they say mercury will make you, but this could just be fatigue.

That girl, she had to die.

You can say her name if you want to, but I don't need to revisit it.

Progress comes with a price. There are sacrifices you have to make. Sometimes, it's as small as getting up from a table and shaking hands and saying goodbye. Leaving some girl sitting there with her poison.

I put two bottles of water and a bag of spice drop candy on the counter. This is a treat, a reward, some little thing like what my father would give me to say I'm doing fine. The clerk is in his middle ages and has soft eyes. His smile is sincere; it only fades after he runs my card through the machine the third time. He says, "I'm very sorry, but it didn't go."

"It wouldn't go through?"

"No, ma'am, I'm sorry."

"I can't imagine why."

He looks at me with his kind eyes worried. Maybe he is about to do something he doesn't want to, but has to. Maybe he is going to take the card the way they do on television and cut it with scissors in front of me. My fear is that I'll react without really wanting to, either, that I'll do something I don't really mean to do. He'll take a pair of scissors from beneath the counter and cut my card and before I can really think it through, I'll have pulled the scissors out of his hands and stuck them in his neck.

I suppose what I mean is that I'm afraid of really and finally snapping.

The man hands me my card back. "Do you have something else to pay with?"

I remember the fifty dollar bill on my car seat, that gift from the man in the forest. "Yes."

I ought to just drive away. I'm not afraid of being on trial or going to prison—that's so unimaginable that I can't believe it is a real possibility.

What I can imagine, what I reasonably fear, is them taking Jack out of the trunk. Them taking Jack away.

I can imagine the man in there making a call right now, whispering into the phone, before he places it gently on the hook and waits for me to come back in.

It's better to keep moving.

But he may not have called. He may know nothing. And if I run, then he'll certainly call.

I snatch up the fifty and march across the lot. I'm just moving through a dream. Anything might happen. It might end now. The man smiles, kindly again, and he makes change.

When I go back out and get into my car and start driving, there is nobody on the road to try to follow or stop me.

I pull onto a little turnoff where a dirt road runs up into the hills. I need to check on Jack.

I've earned this bad idea visit, the way I earned the candy I bought earlier.

It's darkening now. The air is dry and hard to breathe.

In this twilight, Jack looks sort of beautiful amongst all those flowers. What seems like a long time ago, I sometimes admired him while he slept. It was admiration he wanted.

Why was mine not fulfilling for you, Jack?

I wish he could answer, and because of the way we always wish on falling stars, I look up just in case I should be so lucky as to see one tumble now. There are more stars out now than there were when I parked, but it's hard to believe any of them are going to burn out just for me.

I'm startled by an increasingly loud noise, and after a moment I recognize it is the sound of a vehicle coming quickly down the road. It scares me more than it should, as if it is a vehicle driven by someone with a grudge against me. I slam closed the trunk and run up the side of the car and get in quickly. Then I pull back into the dirt road and start forward toward the highway. A set of headlights rounds the bend. For a moment, I can't see what's behind them. Then, that it is an old pickup truck becomes clear.

My car can't speed up enough.

The truck slams into my Mustang. I fly forward and the steering wheel crushes against my chest. I feel my breast bone give a little, the way it did the other night when I braked to a sudden stop. I am aware of other things, the lifting of my ass from the seat, my hair whipping forward across my face.

I am not afraid anymore.

I am simply curious. I wonder what exact part of this accident will result in my death, and I wonder what death will be like. I wonder about blackness and light and sleep and consciousness.

Most importantly, I know that now everything will be okay. It's all over, this life, my potential for pain, all my hope, all my regret, the little joys I'll long for over and over, all of our destinies of loss and disappointment, everything I knew or was going to know, it's just gone.

I'm dead. Honestly, what a relief.

Then my head bounces off of something and the black that flashes is followed immediately by light. Everything seems to spin. Somehow I am half on the floor with my elbow on the passenger side seat. My shoulder is jammed against the dashboard. Nothing hurts.

I know I am not going to die, but I don't feel like moving.

A face appears at the window. It belongs to a teenage boy in a baseball cap. His eyes grow wide, so I can guess I look pretty awful to him. When I raise my hand toward him, he backs out of sight. I wonder if he was really there. Then he comes forward again and pulls the door open. It creaks like a scream that makes me want to cover my ears.

"Are you okay?"

"Yes." My voice sounds strange and so I say it again, trying to make my voice right.

The boy looks toward his truck and then at me again.

I try to get up, and I feel pain for the first time, centered in my shoulder and neck. My head is light. The teenager backs away again, and I use the door to help me stand.

He stares at me. "Can't you put your head up?"

I realize that I have it at an angle. When I try to straighten it, the pain is too much, and so I leave it cocked. "No."

There's a girl standing off to the side. Her face is afraid and she is holding her wrist in her hand, a blond girl with a narrow face, probably fifteen or sixteen, not nearly as pretty as I was then.

"She's bleeding everywhere," the girl says. I look down and see the deep red moving down my dress. I trace the blood up my neck and face, and then I finger the wound. It is a gash, deep, with ragged edges.

"Get her something," the boy says.

The girl waits for a few moments and then walks toward the truck, its driver side panel and hood crumpled. My trunk is half crushed, and I wonder what has happened to Jack in there.

"We weren't drinking," the boy says. "I was driving fast, but we weren't drinking."

"Neither was I."

The girl comes out of the truck with a blue t-shirt. She hands it to the boy and he hands it to me and I wipe my neck and then my face before I dab around the wound.

"What should we do?" the girl asks.

"We have to call the police," the boy says. "It's just an accident. My dad said I'd have one. He said do the right thing. Call the police. I've got insurance. These things are supposed to happen," the boy says. His voice is high and he's been speaking very fast. I feel a little sorry for him.

"It's okay," I say. "You're right. These things are supposed to happen."

"I don't think we're supposed to talk to her," the girl says.

I believe I need to sit, but I try to keep standing.

"Here," the boy says, "Come with me to the truck. You can lay down and we'll drive to town. We'll go to the hospital and then we'll call the police."

The girl shakes her head. "Not in the truck. She's..."

"What?"

"Don't put her in the truck!"

"We got to..."

"We don't have to do anything. She's going to..."

"Shut up!"

"You shut up. She's going to die. Do you want her to die in there?"

The boy glances at me with startled eyes and then drops them away. I have the feeling that he'll never look at me again.

"I'm not going to die," I say. "Not right now." I dab at the wound with the t-shirt again. Then I sit down in my car. My shoulder throbs. My neck hurts. I turn the key. The car starts.

"There," I say. "I can go. I'm not going to die."

"But you're all bloody. Your car is all smashed up."

"It's not bad." I hope that this is true. I hope that Jack is all right in the trunk. This feels like the last hope I can or should have. "I've got to go."

"Take my insurance card. My dad said if I had an accident to give my insurance card."

I try to shake my head but it hurts. The boy disappears and I can hear the truck door opening and closing. Then he comes back with a tattered card that he pushes out toward me. I don't reach for it. He lets it fall in my lap.

"Are you sure you should drive?" he asks.

The girl says, "Let her go. She was out in the middle of the road anyway. She shouldn't have..."

"Close my door."

The boy does it. I put my hands on the wheel. I put my foot on the gas. I can drive. I'm really not going to die.

Pain in my shoulder, pain in my head.

Pain pain pain, I sing it, as if singing it will make it more bearable.

After twenty or thirty miles, there's a rest stop. These are the places bad things happen to people on the road, but I pull in anyway.

I get out of the car and see we're really in the desert now, everything sort of dull orange and dry looking. There's a wind up but even it's warm. I see a soda machine in the little hallway between the bathrooms, but it is unlit and empty looking. A single light burns dimly on a pole and another one beside it has burnt out. It looks like nobody has been here in a long time and like nobody will come here again.

But I am here, and Jack is with me.

I go first into the ladies' room, which smells like dust, and search around for the switch. When I find it, I am half surprised that a light comes on. There is a sheet of polished steel all scratched up for the mirror. My face is distorted in it. There are no paper towels, but in the second stall there is a crushed roll of water-stained toilet paper. I take it off of the holder and, back at the mirror, I do my best to clean the wound on my forehead with a handful of the toilet paper. Fresh blood comes out, and so I tear off three sheets more and stick them over the wound. The blood seeps through and I tear off several more and paste them over the cut. Then I wash my face and I wash my hands.

It is only blood. It is only dirt.

Only only only.

Blood blood blood.

Dirt dirt dirt.

Perhaps I can't get it all off at this moment, but that doesn't matter. There is a bath waiting for me somewhere. I think of those commercials that were on when I was a little girl. The woman would be having a bad day but then she'd take a bubble bath and everything became just fine.

I'd like to be clean. Even if everything still hurt, even if the wounds were still there, I wouldn't mind if I were only clean.

Clean clean clean.

I will be clean.

Writers are supposed to have sleep problems. Writers are supposed to be the kind of people who think and think and think, even into their sleep, perplexed by the big questions of the universe.

But Jack wasn't like that.

Jack, he slept like a baby.

It was me; I was the one who had the insomnia. It got worse the longer I was with him.

The night I killed him—was that three nights ago?—I couldn't sleep.

If you ask me why I couldn't sleep, I might tell you it was because I had been worrying for months, for half our time together, for more than that, about Jack's affection for me. I worried because he'd stopped wanting to fuck me. Because he'd stopped wanting to be close to me even outside of the bedroom.

This was on my mind, and I could say that is why I couldn't sleep. And that is true. But there is more. The truth is, I've never been able to sleep well. Even as a little girl, I'd lie in my bed at night and wish for a button I could push that would put me to sleep.

All my life I've lain awake with restless thoughts running through my head.

It's just that it's been very bad lately.

Jack was already asleep and I was feeling two things about him. The first was a general sense of disgust that bordered on hatred, and I didn't know where that came from, though in hindsight I can see that it probably resulted from this growing suspicion I had that Jack was not as strong or as smart as I'd once thought he was. Despite this repulsion, the second thing I felt for Jack was an overwhelming desire to reconnect with him.

After midnight, I walked into his office, this place I was never supposed to go. I had promised not to read his writings. At first, I thought this meant he believed I wasn't intellectually prepared for them. At first, I told myself that his lack of attention was a kind of prodding, that when he rolled his eyes away from me, that when he showered me with coldness, he was trying to somehow push me toward becoming the person who could understand what he wrote. Who could understand what he thought. That when I'd grown enough, I'd be worthy of understanding him.

I made for him the excuse that he was preparing me. Then, when I was ready, he would bind himself to me in a way that couldn't be undone.

I was in his office because I believed that I would see what there was to be seen of him, even if he thought I wasn't ready. And because I thought that what I'd see would give me faith in him again.

I pushed the button to wake his laptop up. On the screen was the beginning of a novel, and I started to read. It was about a writer. Really, of course, it was about Jack. In the novel, the narrator takes up with a fan who has sent him an email. This is a woman that he saves from a boring relationship with a fat and balding man, and that is really where the novel starts.

At first I thought the girl in the novel couldn't be me, because I was never a fan. I'd never even heard of Jack before the reading, and I didn't even hear him read. The girl looked like me, though, and the man that the narrator saved her from looked like George.

I continued reading. There was a flashback the narrator has of the first time he fucks the fan. He notices that she has a hairy asshole. Because he is turned on in the moment, he pushes the idea of it aside, but he's aware that it will haunt him later.

I know I don't have a hairy asshole, but when I read that part, I had to check. It's harder than it sounds, looking at your asshole. Eventually I gave up on straining around in my bathroom, climbing up on the sink and twisting this way and that, and I got Jack's dental mirror out, thinking, as I slipped it between my legs, about how obsessive he was with his teeth and how he wanted me to be the same way about mine. There wasn't a single hair on or around my asshole.

I took his mirror back.

Jack, he didn't show me his work because he thought I was too stupid to get it. But I got it. The hairy asshole was just a symbol for some fault in a girl a man will get in his mind and never really get out of it. That's not so tough to understand. Nor is it such an insightful thing to write.

I went back to reading.

Just as I thought it would, the symbolic hairy asshole became a point of obsession for the narrator. Though he kept fucking the fan and even let her become his full time lover, he never forgot about his repulsion over the asshole. He told himself that if only it weren't for that, he'd be able to really fall in love with the girl, but for now he couldn't fully put himself in that position.

I got that, too. Jack was trying to say that no matter what, there would be something that would keep the man from fully connecting with the woman.

That's not such a new thing to say. Jack's not the first person to figure that out or to write about it. In fact, it's likely that he just read that idea somewhere else and was just saying it slightly differently now.

That was as far as Jack had gotten. If you asked me, I'd call it pretty mediocre. I didn't see the world differently because of what I read. I hadn't really learned anything.

It all boiled down to this: there was no magic.

That's me in the mirror, thinking about Jack.

Here's what he did wrong:

He didn't love me properly.

He turned out to be a poor writer, and a poor man, for that matter.

He found and fixated on some imperfection in me because that is what he'd do no matter what. Because that was his nature.

And he wrote about this, but he did so without really capturing me.

All of it was pretty lousy, but this last one was what bothered me the most. While I was reading, I kept hoping to read something in it that showed the inside of me, but there was nothing at all, as if he didn't know me. It dawned on me what Jack was really like. He was a person who wanted everybody to know him without himself ever trying to know anybody else. He was in love with himself in a way that made it impossible for him to love anybody else.

I went to where he had fallen asleep in his bathrobe on top of the comforter, waiting for me as he sometimes did before going all he way to bed.

I opened up his bathrobe and looked at the muscles of his chest and his nipples with the stubble of hair sprouting around them. I could see a quiver in his skin where his heart beat. I knew that was the place of what was wrong with him.

It is odd to me that often there is a choice between two things and those things are exactly opposite, but that the chance of you going one way over the other is just fifty-fifty. I was looking down at Jack, feeling for him both love and hate, want and disgust.

What a different story this would be if I'd followed the urge I had to hug him awake. To tell him I wanted to be his forever, whoever he was, however small, whatever it meant, just him and me. It was a desire to say everything so earnestly and finally that whoever hears it has to melt toward you.

But that's not what I did.

And it's all right if sometimes I wish I had.

What I did was pick up the ball-shaped glass paperweight he kept on the windowsill, a blue ball, heavy with little bubbles trapped in the glass. I walked over and thought for a moment more about how bad his novel was and how little he knew me or ever would and how little really he was even though he tried to pretend he was more, and I brought the ball down as hard as I could on the place where his skin was pulsing with the beat of his heart.

He gasped. The sound of it made me angrier

Jack half sat up. "What's wrong? What's happening?"

He pushed himself to standing and wobbled forward and looked at me for the first time, trying to focus his eyes. He reached for the light switch, which he missed once and then twice before clicking it on. "Something is wrong," he said, his voice airy.

He touched his chest and then looked at his hand. The flesh had grown bright red over his heart, but no blood had come through and it looked like some awful birthmark on his pale skin.

He looked at me, his mouth opening and closing.

I backed away.

He started toward me, taking staggering steps and putting his hand to his chest. "Call the police," he said.

He moved his hand from his chest to my arm. I swung again, bringing the glass ball into his solar plexus. He let out a wheeze and I hit again, this time catching the area of his heart. He staggered backward and then he slumped forward. His face came toward mine, his eyes squeezed closed, as if he were moving in for a kiss.

Then his mouth opened and his awful breath poured out.

I backed away again, until I was against the wall, and he sank to his knees, putting his hands on his thighs and turning his head from side to side, looking like our dog did when I was a kid and it got hit by a car and came up into the yard to die.

I brought the ball down on his back in the place I thought his heart would be and I felt something break inside of him. He crumpled to the floor and his legs kicked and I watched them until they stilled.

I thought then it was time to stop.

As I started for the door, Jack slowly turned himself over and looked up at me. For a moment I felt tender toward him, and so I went and knelt beside him. He said my name. One of his eyes was closing and unclosing like he was winking and the other one was wide open. "Why?" he said.

Maybe he really didn't know.

I smashed the ball down on his chest. He let out a cough or something like it. And I hit him again and again, but nothing more seemed to give away.

I stopped to breathe.

When I put my hand against the area I had been hitting, I could feel how all the muscle and skin had gone pulpy. His heart was beating, but strangely.

Using my fist, I beat on his chest a dozen times, and then I hit it with the ball two or three more times.

Now I was exhausted and he still was breathing, not even fully unconscious. "Please," he gasped. "Why?"

I got up and looked through the window. It was purely dark out there. I went into the kitchen and poured some chocolate soy milk. As I drank it, I wondered if I'd really done what I remembered doing or if it was all some lack of sleep dream, the way since then sometimes I'll wonder what is real and what isn't, even though in my heart, I know it's all real. I went back in the bedroom and saw that Jack had gotten to his hands and knees and was crawling, not going toward the phone or the doorway, but just moving, as if to prove to himself that he could. It was grotesque. I kicked my foot up into the place I'd been hitting, a good kick, one that lifted him a little and then caused him to slump forward.

When I rolled him over, I saw that a fist sized area on his chest looked like a blood blister. With the glass ball, I hit it as hard as I could. The blister area popped and blood spurted out.

I knew right then everything that was going to happen. I knew I was going to take his body and put it in the trunk, and I knew I was going to start driving. I even knew I was going to find George and that I was going to live happily ever after with him.

I went to my bathroom and washed myself clean of the blood. Then I put on some moisturizer and I brushed my teeth. I wetted a towel, and when I started to clean the blood off of Jack's face, one of his eyes opened.

"Jack?"

Bloody spit came up in his mouth. He was trying to tell me something. For just a moment, I felt sorry for him. I felt like it was okay that he was weak and that maybe now that he knew I knew it, we could be together. I believed he might be saved. I could drive him to a hospital and they could fix him up and then I'd take care of him. He'd never take me for granted again.

But I realized this was just a fairy tale.

I put my hand and over his mouth and nose. His body began to wiggle. I could feel how desperate his breath was to get out. Finally a stream of it broke through and then he sucked in some air. I let go.

I put my hand on the broken flesh above his heart and leaned down with all my strength so that I could feel the sternum bend in. By putting my feet on the bed, I was able to get almost the whole weight of my body on him. His entire torso felt to be sinking inward. When I didn't have the energy to hold myself like that anymore, I picked up the ball and just began hitting and hitting.

Maybe he was dead before I'd started, but he was certainly dead before I'd finished.

I cleaned the rest of his face. I went back and washed my face and hands again. Then I half expected him to be alive as he was before, but he was not.

He really was not.

He really was dead.

He really is.

Using several towels, I sopped the blood off of his chest and no more came out. Then I put a sheet in the trunk of the Mustang. I went back and I closed Jack's bathrobe and tied it. Then I began dragging him. When I got him in the trunk, I folded the sheet over his face, which made me feel clean somehow.

I didn't want to go back into the apartment at all. But I knew I need my makeup case and my toothbrush and a tube of toothpaste. I grabbed my purse and I took another dress and a few pairs of panties and that was all. I shut off the lights and I locked the door.

That was it.

I killed Jack and I started toward George.

Now here I am some exact place that I don't know exactly. Still, I am sure I'm close, in the desert of Utah or maybe Oregon, with Washington State not far away. With Seattle a makeable distance. With my own blood on my face. With Jack still in the trunk.

This restroom bathroom with my eyes closed very tightly.

George, he's sleepwalking through his life, waiting for the proper girl to come and wake him up, waiting for me, even if he doesn't know it. He will take me into his soft arms, against his soft belly. All he needs to do to save us is find a way to bond me to him so that I never want to leave again.

I picture him as best I can.

Then I open my eyes and see my face in that sheet of steel. Even though the reflection is stretched and my face is smeared with blood and dirt, I see clearly. What I see is that I'm lying to myself.

What I see is that George cannot save me. George cannot fulfill me.

I have not changed in that way. I wanted to, but I just didn't.

There is too much that I need. There is too much that I want. Somebody would have to carve away at me, some doctor with a scalpel in my brain, some preacher with the threat of fire in my soul; they'd have to cut and burn me into another woman

Decomposition

altogether. Without that, I'll never stick to a man like George, no matter how much I want to be the kind of woman who can.

So this mistake, this is big.

So I ought to just collapse, right here on this bathroom floor. Give it up, because what is there, really, to move forward with?

Before I tumble, something catches me.

It's Jack.

I've reached my final epiphany, and the only person I want to tell is him.

And that I'm sorry.

Everything is visible now. What a hard journey to clarity. But here I am.

Jack, I came to you.

The trunk is smashed in such a way that I can't even get the key in the lock. I stick my hands beneath the rim and try to pull the lid up. My nails break and my finger tips tear, and the lid does not budge.

The tire iron I left inside after breaking the thermometer. How I wish I had it now.

I have changed.

I have learned.

And now this trunk is stuck, and if only it weren't.

I throw the roses out of the backseat. I can't get the upholstery off, and so I smash the back passenger side window with a rock. Then I dig around in the broken glass for a piece I can grip. I cut into the upholstery, ignoring the feeling that my palms and fingers are being cut until I've completed an "x," and then I put my hands beneath the dome light.

For a moment, I just stare.

I had beautiful hands. They will be beautiful again. Everything can be repaired.

It will take a month to put me back together. It will take hairdressers and manicurists and dermatologists and God knows what else.

But it can be done.

Everything can.

What you destroy, you can rebuild.

If you can kill, you can unkill. That only just makes sense.

I rip apart the upholstery and I tear out the stuffing. A metal sheet stands between me and Jack. I beat against it with the rock, but all I get is the clunking sound.

Thunk thunk thunk. Like some drum that starts up in some old movie when you know something bad is going to happen.

I get out and yell as loudly as I can. I haven't meant to scream anything in particular, but as it echoes away from me, I realize that what I screamed is: Help!

There is nobody in this quiet dark to answer.

I will not despair. I will not give in.

My real happy ending is in sight. This is the final test.

I walk around to the trunk again, and there I lie down on the ground so that I can crawl a little ways beneath the back of the car. Jack's right over me now. Everything will work out. I know how this fairy tale ends. I'm tired and not thinking properly, so right now this final puzzle is a bit beyond me, but I'll get it.

The answer is right here.

I will sleep and wake stronger of body and mind. Then I will find a way to open the trunk.

I will lean in and kiss you, Jack, and you will come awake.

THE END

Epilogue

By Susannah Breslin

This is the story about the year I killed a man, put him in my trunk, and drove across the country. Of course, that all happened a long time ago. Now, things are different for me. At least, that's what I told myself. Then, I got this book, the one you're holding in your hands, and I wasn't so sure anymore. It all came back to me: how it happened, why it happened, and it was like it was happening all over again. It was like it was happening to someone else who was both me and not me at the same time.

These days, though, the difference between reality and fiction makes no difference to me—but, that's another story altogether, isn't it? I was sitting on the porch, after the hurricane, after I had killed that life, after he was dead and gone, when it was delivered to me. This book was sitting in the palms of my hands, lying right in front of me, like another dead body, like a person who wanted to be read, like some kind of thing demanding I perform a vivisection on it with my eyes, or my soul, or my heart, or some something I wasn't even sure I had. It's hard to say, or know, or think what I thought when I saw what it was I had.

Personally, I do not believe there is one of us among us who has not killed another one of us like I did. The difference with me is it was real. So, this book is like a cemetery that lives inside my mind, the pages are like tombstones that haunt me today, and the only thing I can't figure out is if George is still alive, if Jack is the one whose body I'm supposed to find, or if it's me somewhere beneath the leaves, under six feet of dirt, strewn in a million pieces at the base of an old oak tree felled by a storm 500 miles wide.

There are a lot of stories that aren't in here, I can tell you that. The one about the prison that was like my own private panopticon, the one about the woman who had a gun in her pants bigger than the one in my mouth, the one about how it felt when

I drove out of the last place I ever left in my life. No one was there with me when I looked up into the sky above me, hanging over all those trees destroyed by something I could not see, and there was something inside my trunk that was too terrible for me to even begin to describe.

That's when I saw something that was bigger than me, that was bigger than this world, that was bigger than all of us. In that moment, it was like I knew nothing, it was like I knew everything, and it was like I knew what I had to do was close my eyes, I had to leave that life, and I had to go another way. I let Jesus take the wheel, I let Satan drive for awhile, or maybe it was me who was the one it had to be who did it.

A long time after that, I changed my name, I walked off the edge of the world, and I disappeared. I thought what I had done was dead and gone. This book is proof someone found me, someone knows I'm here, someone I don't know if I am or if I am someone I am not anymore. I can't tell. Can you? Maybe. All I ask is you look inside this book the way I looked inside that trunk. I hope you find me under the guise of someone else's name telling a story that is neither theirs nor mine nor yours but all of ours instead. Remember what it's like when you get to the end, you stop, and you can hear the sound of your own heart beating. Because that heart, you see, is all mine.

About The Author

Author of the short story collection *Animal Rights and Pornography*, J Eric Miller lives and teaches creative writing in Colorado. He doesn't eat, amongst other things, chicken.

Printed in the United States
117612LV00001B/40/A